IRA TABANKIN

NATO'S ARTICLE 5 GAMBIT
BOOK 3

INTO THE DARKNESS

NATO's Article 5 Gambit
Book 3
Into The Darkness

Copyright September 2023.
Ira J. Tabankin
Knoxville, TN 39720
Cover by 100 Covers

Dedication:
This book is dedicated to my wife and true love, Patricia.

Thanks:
I want to thank my beta readers, who helped me with their knowledge, comments, and encouragement. I'd like to thank Stuart Budgen and Gary Neely who edited and made this edition possible.

Note:
Please note this isn't a politically correct novel. Please recognize that artistic license is used throughout this story. Any tense disparities are the author's view of the story as it's written.

Work of Fiction:
This is a work of fiction. Names, characters, businesses, places, events, and incidents are either the products of the author's imagination or used in a fictitious manner. Any resemblance to actual persons, living or dead, or actual events is purely coincidental.

A Note on Punctuation:
Much of this story is a conversation between people; when we speak, we don't do so in the same manner as the written word. Pauses in the written word aren't usually there when we talk to each other. As such, the punctuation used in conversations is written as people speak, not as it would be in a written paragraph.

Note on names.

The names of the leaders of the respective countries in this story are the same, and all of the supporting staff have fictional names.

Prologue

The war with Russia was over and I guess you could say that we won. How is victory measured though, you might ask? Would it be the side that lost the most, lost the war? Or is the winner the side that managed to retain its soul? Or who even still has a soul after a nuclear war? Millions died in the quick and comparatively painless way. One moment they were alive and the next, they were vapor tossed around in a nuclear fireball.

The unlucky ones died from radiation poisoning, many having no idea what they were even suffering from. Deadly fallout was carried by the winds and it contaminated millions of acres of land. Millions who lived far away from the primary targets didn't even know they had received a fatal dose until it was too late.

Many of the people who knew the score were obliged to take the lives of their children to save them from suffering before they took their own lives. I'm a Christian, but is taking the lives of your children in their sleep so they pass without pain a sin? Is taking one's own life a sin when you already know you are doomed?

Millions didn't have the luxury of contemplating the question. As loving parents, they just couldn't bear to see their children or aged parents suffer the horrible certain death that is guaranteed through radiation poisoning. Many mixed all of their prescription drugs into a 'drug cocktail' and prayed their loved ones would pass in their sleep. Others weren't fortunate enough to have a medicine chest full of deadly medications, so they resorted to a single shot in the back of their loved ones' heads – messy but foolproof. This was usually followed by placing their guns in their own mouths and blowing their heads apart. Again, messy but foolproof.

Many of those who survived the Hell on Earth that was the nuclear holocaust prayed for death. All of the things they took for granted were gone, there was no clean water, food was at a premium, and basic medications were unavailable. Those who required medications for their survival didn't stand a chance.

There was still a President. He had previously been the Speaker of the House, and the title of President had passed from the former President to the Vice President, both of whom had died in the initial strikes on the Capital. The Speaker of the House had been on a plane on his way from his home district in California to Washington when the 'balloon' went up.

His plane had set down at the first surviving base they located: Fort Huachuca. One of the President's aides knew of a safe place where they could reestablish the capital. It was centrally located and underground. He showed the President an article about the Subtropolis: a series of mines under Kansas City. The President liked the idea and ordered me, a lowly Major who had been frocked to the position of General in the disaster that was the Ukraine war, to take care of making it happen, shortly after the ship that brought us home from the radioactive ashes that was now Europe.

My frocking was made permanent and, lacking anyone else, I was also named the new Secretary of Defense. My best friend, who had tried to hide his radiation poisoning from me, became my executive assistant. We were tasked with finding a safe route that the new government could use to relocate and rebuild under Kansas City. I appointed a young Captain, as I knew his uncle and figured if Captain Rand was anything like him, he was the leader I needed to take on this mission.

I had also appointed Captain Karen Gold to find a way to cross the Mississippi River and secure the mines in Indiana that were used to store millions of MREs and millions of pounds of cheese. I don't understand the cheese, but food was food. Starving people will eat anything, and sometimes even each other.

I pitied both of them because I knew they had a dirty mission. I had no sooner dispatched them than we received word that the Cartels had managed to get their hands on nuclear weapons. The Texas Rangers asked for our help in dealing with it. I should have seen the trap in the request because Texas had actually been planning to break away from the Union and use nukes to blackmail us.

I recalled Captain Gold when it became clear Rand was going to need more manpower than he had. He was up against a smart and cold-hearted Warlord; yes, a warlord right here in America. Captain Gold's convoy was ambushed, and she was captured by the Warlord to be used as a bargaining chip. Now things were going to turn very dark; the midday sun soon to resemble something more akin to midnight.

Chapter 1

Captain Gold floated on a raft in a warm swimming pool. She felt that she didn't have a care in the world. She liked the feeling of the warm sun on her body as she daydreamed while floating in the pool. There weren't any waves to interfere with her nap. Her Legs and arms hung over the sides of the inflatable raft and dipped into the tepid water beneath her. She dreamt of the small beagle she had when she was eight. She really loved that little brown and black pooch with a white stripe that ran down its head between its eyes. She walked it all over her small neighborhood. She thought the dog's name had been OQ, and she smiled as she remembered it was an unusual name for a dog.

She heard her mother calling her. "Karen, Karen, where's your puppy? Where's little OQ? Honey, why did you name it OQ? Does it mean something special to you? Please tell me what it means. It's driving me crazy trying to understand why you gave that little puppy such a strange name.

I'm sure you had a reason for it. I promise I won't tell your brother or father. It will be our little secret."

Karen Gold drifted on her raft and struggled to answer her mother. She loved her mother, but she couldn't bring herself to tell her why she had given her dog such a strange name. She mouthed the letters, "OQ." But there wasn't any sound coming from her lips. She tried to remember why she'd picked such an unusual name, but she just couldn't remember.

The Warlord, Captain Sharon Letts stood on the right side of the medical examination table that Captain Gold was strapped to. Gold had an IV in each arm, and wires wrapped around her head, chest, and ankles. A 3D video helmet was placed on her head, covering her eyes so she only saw what the programmers wanted her to see and feel. They had tried to bring her back to her childhood in an effort to get around the mental block that stopped her from telling Letts what the two-letter code meant.

Gold was wearing a standard medical robe. Her body was covered with a fine layer of sweet-smelling sweat. A tech gently moved a strand of Gold's hair from her forehead. "Ma'am, she's under as deep as we can put her. She's trying to answer the question. Either she really doesn't know the answer, or her mind has a block on it."

Letts shook her head; she was angry, and it showed on her face. She spoke out loud so the techs could hear her frustration. "Why would someone have placed a block in her memory? What the hell could 'OQ' mean? I've asked every intelligence agent we have, and no one has any idea. I've placed the home guard on alert so many times that I'm afraid they'll revolt if I sound the alarm again and it proves to be a false sighting. I wouldn't be surprised if the people strung me up by a rope until I'm dead if I keep waking them up in the middle of the night." Letts looked at the soldier strapped to the table, "I don't think she can handle another dose of the crap we got from those asshole Chinese. I'd like to use it on the doctor who sold it to me. All that gold and silver for nothing."

The tech looked at the monitors and then touched Gold's neck. "Ma'am, she is strong. She can handle another dose. Should I prepare it?"

Letts studied the woman on the table and slowly shook her head. "I don't think the drugs are having any effect on her. We may have to resort to different measures to unlock her memory. I need to know what 'OQ' means at any cost. Does it mean all is clear and we can proceed with our attack plans, or does it mean they know what we're up to?" She turned toward the tech. "Slowly wake her. Do NOT harm her. I need her in good shape if we're going to use her as a bargaining chip. For now, that includes her mind. I may decide to use the stronger drugs on her, but for now, I want her in perfect shape in case we have to provide proof of life." Letts was almost out of the room when she turned and looked at the two techs again. "No harm means do not abuse her. If I find out you broke my orders and screwed around with her, I'll hook you to your own machine and give you the worst nightmares the programmers can think of... and we have a few real sickos on the staff. They'll make you feel like you've been impaled on a long pole up your ass. So don't harm her."

The senior tech, shook from fear, said, "Ma'am, if you resort to the other means, it will leave marks, both physical and mental. She could be permanently harmed. I thought the plan was to make sure she wasn't marked or harmed in any way. I believe those were your orders."

Letts stared at the tech while she whipped her sidearm out and shot him in the groin. Now you won't need any surgery because I've shot your balls off." She smiled at what she'd just done. She considered him to be a little asshole anyway. The wounded tech was dragged away while someone began to clean the blood off of the floor.

She leered at the remaining techs in the lab. "We can inflict enough pain to break her memory lock without leaving any permanent marks, so when we finally trade her, they will only have to worry about her having more than a few nightmares. They'll place her in some kind of mental care, by which time it will be too late for them anyway. We'll have launched our attack and defeated them. Then, I will enjoy watching her slowly go insane while we torture her lover in front of her. But before that can happen, we have to break her so I know what the code means. In fact, I changed my mind, hit her with another shot of the crap you developed. If I can't pull the answer from her, maybe I'll decide that she'll live her life out in a dream world of suffering."

The tech pulled out a small bottle and injected it into the bag of clear fluid connected to Gold's right arm. "Sweet dreams asshole."

Gold floated on the raft in bliss. She felt the weather changing. All of a sudden, everything changed. In a flash, she felt like she was inside an uninsulated tent with Rand, who suggested they get undressed and seal themselves in the warm sleeping bag. Gold was utterly unaware that everything she was experiencing was simply thoughts that were inserted directly into her brain. She looked to the horizon and saw a wall of snow being driven by a massive winter storm coming her way.

*****

Major Rand had been up for thirty-six hours straight, and he was physically and mentally exhausted. He was depressed and very worried about the fact that he hadn't heard a word from Captain Gold or her convoy. The scouts reported they had been under orders to only use their radio for a quick burst when they arrived at the FOB.

Rand asked them what they had been ordered to burst. "Sir, we were given two codes, one meant we made it here without any problems and the other that we had seen an indication of a potential ambush. We got delayed on the freeway due to some rough weather, but we didn't see any of Letts' troops, so we sent the all-clear code." Rand forgot to ask what the codes were. He just assumed they were the same as the ones he had his squads use.

Rand tried to hide a yawn. He couldn't remember the last time he'd slept more than a short cat nap. He looked at his staff, all of whom looked as tired as he felt, and he said, "Keep looking for Captain Gold's convoy. Her scouts made it here, but her convoy disappeared. I want them found. My gut is telling me that that bitch Letts pulled off an ambush and either captured the convoy or destroyed it. I don't think she's stupid enough to harm Captain Gold though. If I had to guess, I'd say she's going to hold the captain hostage to stop us from going after her."

Rand covered his mouth trying to hold another yawn in. "I think this is a perfect time to use the new drones. As a matter of fact, you have permission to use every asset we have. I want her found. I don't know what Letts wants, but I'm sure she'll let us know soon enough. I'd like to have an idea before she drops it on us. Whatever she has on her little mind, I want – I NEED – to know what it is so I know how to respond. I know you're all as beat as I am, but please look under every rock, use every HUMINT asset we have, and take advantage of every snooping device in our inventory. The Secretary gave us those new toys, so get busy putting them to good use. I need some sleep. I want a full brief when I wake in say, four hours, but wake me sooner if you learn anything of importance."

Rand fell into a deep and exhaustive sleep. He slept in his uniform in case something happened, and he was needed in the command center, so it would save him the couple of minutes it would take him to get dressed. He kept a coffee machine running around the clock, so he always had a mug of coffee when he woke or was working late. A mess corporal was assigned to make sure the pot was always fresh. No one wanted to face Rand without his coffee.

Rand was so tired he quickly entered REM sleep and began dreaming of his youth. *He remembered his mother screaming and crying when on 9/11/2001 two airplanes struck the World Trade Towers. He remembered his mother saying it was like Pearl Harbor again and America was at war.*

"Mommy, war like the one Papa fought in? Against the Koreans again?"

"No, honey, this is different. This was an attack because as a country we won't accept their view of the Bible."

"Mommy, I don't understand, isn't there one Bible? I don't understand how there could be more than one. Father Murphy told us the Bible was the word of God. Why would God have written different Bibles?" Before Rand's mother could answer the phone rang. It was one of her friends who called to say that the Pentagon had been hit too. Mom screamed because her brother, my Uncle Harry was at the Pentagon.

Rand's mind drifted back to when his uncle had taken him to the Pentagon. *My uncle had taken him there twice. He was a LTC in the US Army. Uncle Harry took me along with him because he wasn't married and didn't have any children, so he took me to the annual 'Bring your sons and daughters to work day.' We lived in Sterling, Virginia and he lived in Arlington. He was Mom's older brother. I don't know how much older since Mom said her age was a secret and children shouldn't know their mother's age.*

Uncle Harry picked me up at what he called 0530. What a funny way to tell time. I told him my watch didn't say 0530, it showed 5:30. He rubbed my head and explained the twenty-four-hour clock. I felt so grown up, I remember when we got home, I told Mom what time it was in twenty-four time saying it was eighteen-fifteen hours. Mom asked me to clean up while she had a little chat with Uncle Harry. I didn't tell Mom my mind was made up that day, I wanted to be like Uncle Harry. I wanted to wear a neat uniform like his. I wanted those colorful little rows of badges he wore on the left side of his chest. I liked the way his shoes gleamed, and I was so embarrassed by how dirty my white Nikes looked.

Uncle Harry showed me a room that was filled with large TVs and people either called him Sir or he called others Sir. He tried to explain ranks and salutes to me, but even after three times I was still confused. I was also confused because everyone talked in a funny language. I couldn't understand most of the words they spoke. I learned as I got older that I was hearing made-up words from the abbreviations they had for everything. They even had funny names for places like the bathrooms. One of Uncle Harry's people called the bathroom a 'head.' I was told it was what they called bathrooms on ships and that that person was a sailor, but I thought Uncle Harry was in the Army. By fifteen hundred hours, my head hurt. I couldn't keep track of all the new things I heard about.

I enjoyed my days with my uncle, and then on 9/11 Mom learned the Pentagon had been hit and she couldn't reach Uncle Harry. She broke down crying. Two hours later, Colonel Watts, Uncle Harry's boss called to tell her that her brother had been injured in the attack. He said that Uncle Harry was a hero, because even wounded he had saved four people from the burning building. He told her that Uncle Harry was being sent to a hospital and he would let her know when she could visit him.

It took a couple of hours for her to tell me that Uncle Harry had been injured in the attack on the Pentagon. I didn't understand how he, the bravest man I knew, could have been injured by anything, and then Mom showed me the pictures of the smoking Pentagon and reminded me that Uncle Harry's office was behind that smoke. Mom told me the airplane struck the Pentagon where Uncle Harry's office had been. All but two of his staff died when the plane hit the building. We later learned that even though his left leg was broken and he was burned, he had carried two people out of the burning building and then he limped back in to bring two more to safety before the pain was too great for him to bear and he laid on the grass until a medic found him. They loaded him on a helicopter that took him to the hospital.

Three weeks later, Mom and I drove to Maryland to visit Uncle Harry in the hospital. Half of his face was covered in white bandages and there was a small tent over his legs. Mom broke down when she saw him like that.

Uncle Harry opened his arms and hugged us. He told us he would be okay and that when the injury healed, he would get a new leg. At the time I didn't understand. Mom explained it to me on the way home. The doctors couldn't save his broken leg. The bone had been shattered, and parts of it were sticking out of his calf. The surgeons had removed his left leg below his knee.

Twelve weeks later, Uncle Harry came for Sunday dinner.

I was shocked at how he looked. His normal brown hair was mostly gray. There were lines on his face that hadn't been there when I had seen him in the hospital. The left side of his face was scarred and still pink. He had to use crutches to get around. He only had one shoe on. Mom had warned me not to say anything. He and Mom had a long talk, and when he left, I saw my mother cry till she shook.

It was the second time I remembered her crying that hard. The first was a year ago when the police officers told her Daddy had been hit by a drunk driver and didn't make it. I cried too and I didn't want to come out of my room. Mom told me we had to learn to live without him. That may have been easy for her to say, but later I learned how hard it was for her to actually put it into practice.

Uncle Harry visited us every couple of weeks. He told us what had happened, and how he'd been injured and still carried two of his people out of the burning building. Time passed and he eventually received his new leg. He learned to walk and even run again. I made a silent promise to myself that when I grew up, I was going to hunt down and kill those who'd hurt my uncle.

When I was sixteen, and Uncle Harry had returned from his second deployment from the Global War on Terror (GWOT) he took me out to lunch and asked me what I thought I wanted to do when I grew up. I looked into his eyes and told him I wanted to hurt those who'd hurt him and our country. I told him I wanted to kill all of them.

He smiled and helped me make a plan. I worked hard to make him proud. Mom wasn't happy with my choice, because she didn't want to bury her husband and her son. I promised her she wouldn't have to. Boy, was I dumb. Uncle Harry carried a lot of weight in the Army. He was now a Major General, had a chest full of war-earned decorations, and was friends with our Senator. I quickly learned I was going to West Point. I had a fire inside of me; a fire that drove me to be the best and to avenge my uncle.

I was a loner for most of my four years at West Point, focusing all of my energy on being the best. I had worked out at home and at a gym every day to prepare my body and mind for the tests I knew lay ahead of me. I remember when my middle school friends played games, I planned how to kill terrorists. I also made both the football and the fencing teams, and when graduation came, I was fifth of my class. I was wooed by every department, but I surprised all of them when I chose the infantry. I wanted to follow in my uncle's footsteps.

Uncle Harry told me he was bursting with pride over my accomplishments. I went to infantry school and then reported to Fort Benning as a shiny new Gold 'butter' Bar LT. Most thought I didn't know shit, but they quickly learned who my uncle was and that I was the real deal. Uncle Harry had taught me to rely on and learn from my sergeants and to always assume I was wrong, and they were right. He told me that the best officers listened to their sergeants, and I was a fast learner. I was also quickly promoted, I assumed that Uncle Harry, now a LT General, had a small bit to do with that. I had spent two years following in my uncle's footsteps. I fought at the end of the War on Terror, but we were screwed by our government, who had given us ROEs that resulted in many of my friends being wounded and some killed. After returning from Afghanistan, I attended a few additional schools and then I left for Mexico. We'd finally thought about stopping the Cartels. It was then that LT Gold and my paths crossed.

I met Karen Gold during our joint time at Jump School, which I had been sent to after a nine-month stint in Mexico. I was surprised and pleased she had decided to become jump qualified. When I asked her about it, her eyes sparkled as she told me, "I think even if I never get a chance to jump into a combat situation, the jump companies are the ones who deploy into the world's hot spots first, and frankly I didn't sign up to man a desk or spend my days typing reports no one will read. I want to see action."

I smiled at her, thinking that if she ever knew what real combat felt like she wouldn't want it. I wondered how she would respond when the bullets flew and when she lost the first soldier under her command. I'll never forget the time Private Jones, or what was left of him, lay in my arms bleeding out. There weren't enough bandages to seal his wounds from the damn Cartels' mortar rounds. They got the damn things from the Mexican Army who got them from who? From us. Mexico was a real cluster F—k and now we were preparing to jump into Columbia. That was the hornet's nest of Central America.

Rand tossed and turned in his sleep, dreaming of his time with Karen. He remembered the heat he felt every time he got the opportunity to spend some time with her. He quickly realized he was attracted to her, and after the balloon went up, he had the opportunity to rekindle his feelings for her. Only now he knew he couldn't act on those feelings because Captain Gold was under his command. That meant he had to be professional. He briefly woke to check his watch, then he rolled over and fell back into a deep sleep thinking of her.

Three hours after he'd laid down, his Top Sergeant banged on the door. "Sir, I have some information concerning Captain Gold."

Chapter 2

Rand jumped up from his cot. "Reynolds, is that you?"

"Yes, sir. We have some new intel."

"Give me a minute. I'll meet you at my office."

"I'll have breakfast waiting for you. I know how you are when you're hungry."

Rand had taken a few minutes to wash, shave, and change uniforms before he entered the headquarters building and his office. True to Top's word, a tray with eggs, bacon, toast, and three pancakes, plus a pot of hot coffee was steaming under a clear plastic cover. "My, we're getting fancy. You must have some very bad news. Hit me with it."

"Sir beats MREs for breakfast. I swear whoever decided on eggs in an MRE without any hot sauce should have been forced to live on the rotten things. Eat a little and then we can review the intel. It isn't going anywhere, and you need your strength."

Rand nodded. "Now I know it's bad news. Speaking of the asshole who put powdered eggs in our MREs, I bet he died in the war. If he didn't then I agree with you." Rand dug into his breakfast. "Okay, I feel human, tell me the bad and then the good news, in that order."

Reynolds knew the intel was going to be bad news so he poured himself another mug of coffee. "Sir, we sent a couple of drones along the freeway used by Captain Gold's scouts. They told us the convoy was supposed to follow the same route. The drones discovered the remains of Captain Gold's convoy hidden under some camo: cut down branches and ground junk, leaves, cut brushes, you name it."

"How did they discover them?"

"Thermal and imagine match, they didn't do a good job covering them. We got lucky, the drone was able to match a fender and a wheel with our trucks."

"Is that the good or the bad news? Have we put any boots on the ground?"

"Sir, it's just the news. So far, we haven't discovered any bodies. We haven't sent any boots on the ground yet. We just received the news, and I wanted you to make the decision about sending boots when it could be an ambush. Sir, Sergeant Elliot is in command of today's response squad."

"Ask him to see me, and while you're at it, send the SOB scout leader to see me. I think it's past time he and I had a little chat. Something about his story bothers me."

Reynolds asked, already knowing the answer, "Sir, here or?"

"Bring him to the front door. He and I are going to have a little walk. I am going to find out everything he knows. There's something about his story that doesn't ring right. If he and the three other scout trucks had done their jobs, there's no way Captain Gold's convoy could have driven into an ambush. In fact, I want the scouts placed in protective custody. My gut is telling me that at least one of them is a spy."

Sergeant Reynolds silently nodded his head. "Sir, what if one or more gives us trouble?"

Rand looked at Reynolds. "Do I really have to answer that?"

Before Reynolds could answer, a radio operator came running toward them. "Major, the President is on the line. He's asking for you."

Rand looked at Reynolds. "Can this day start off any better?"

Reynolds nodded. "Sir, you had real eggs and bacon for breakfast."

"You've got a point there. You'd better get the camp ready to move. I have a bad feeling the President is going to light a fire under us to get our butts to Kansas City. I really don't want to leave without finding Captain Gold, but he is the Commander in Chief."

President McCarthy was smooth as silk to Major Rand, telling him how he knew the clock had run down and he was going to have to find the safe road to Kansas City. He wished the President would fly, but after his plane had to crash land at the base when it was hit by the EMP from the Russian nukes, he knew he preferred to stay on the ground. Rand's mission had started with him plotting a safe route to the caves and then providing security for the new government while it set up business in the massive mines.

Rand began by saying, "Mr. President, I would like to thank you for allowing us the time to search for Captain Gold and her people. I recognize that speed is of the utmost importance to secure the mines so you can take the next steps in reforming the government."

"Major, well put. When do you plan on leaving?"

"Sir, I was planning on first light tomorrow. We have drone footage of what we believe is the remains of Captain Gold's convoy."

"Major, were you able to locate the captain or any survivors?"

"No, sir."

"I see. I am going to get with the Secretary, and we'll send a Delta Squad to search the area."

"Mr. President, I don't mean to talk out of school, but the Warlord's people are well-trained and put up a hell of a fight. They broke into at least five National Guard armories and now have all of their weapons and gear. I think we should send more than one squad."

The President paused, as Rand heard him talking to someone who was listening but not taking an active part in the call. Rand waited for the President to come back on the phone. "Major, it's been suggested to me that you take a few additional days to clear up the mystery of Captain Gold. Major, I don't believe in leaving people behind. Get to the bottom of our missing captain, and if possible, terminate the Warlord. Major, we can't afford to lose your command so don't fall into one of their traps. Major, I can give you five days, but not another second, am I clear?"

Rand replied, "Yes, sir. Thank you, sir."

"I want a report every night at 6 PM."

"Yes, sir."

Rand walked out of the radio room hiding the smile he felt as Sergeant Reynolds approached him. "Major, when do we leave?"

"In five days. He gave us five days to locate Captain Gold. He and the Secretary are sending us a Delta Squad to help locate the captain and her people. I'm wound up, so it's time to have my favorite kinds of discussions with the scout leader. Where is he?"

"Sir, he's waiting for you in front of your office."

"What about the rest of the scouts?"

"Sir, let's say they're not lonely."

Reynolds racked a live round into his M7 and smiled at Rand. "Sir, I have a new M17 in my truck if you'd like one."

"Thank you, but I have my M17." Rand pulled it from his pack and attached the drop holster and racked a round. Reynolds looked at the ammo in the magazines.

Reynolds looked at the magazine Rand showed him, "JHP? I thought we were only supposed to use FMJ rounds."

"Sergeant, I don't think there is a Geneva anymore so screw them and their silly rule about FMJ rounds. I have a few boxes in my office if you would like some?"

Reynolds smiled and pulled his loaded magazine from the handset of his M17. "Sir, do you mean like these?"

"Yup, just like those." Both men laughed. Reynolds said, "If I'm going to put a hole in someone, I want it to be a large one and not one that just zips through. I assume you made sure everyone who carries a M17 has the JHP rounds."

"Yes, sir. Remember that large gun store we checked out a week or so ago? I helped us to some of their inventory."

Rand smiled, "I did too."

Both men smiled at each other. Rand said, "Use the FMJ rounds for practice and make sure every M17 is loaded with the JHP rounds."

"Yes, sir."

"I'm going to take a little with the scout. I don't trust him. Is the 'box' ready for us when, or if, he returns from our walk?"

"It will be. The special platoon is setting it up in the portable SCIF."

"Excellent. I'll see you soon."

"I'll be right behind you in case you need backup."

*****

Today is going to be one of the saddest days of my life. I'm General Tom Morton, and up until six months ago I was a simple staff major for the First Armor Division deployed to Ukraine. We were deployed as part of NATO's Article 5 response. Russia had, and I believed them when they said it, a targeting error that had caused a few of their missiles to strike and explode on Polish soil. The leaders of Poland declared they were under attack, and they were demanding that NATO agree to support their claim of Article 5 that in simple language said, an attack on one was an attack on all.

NATO had provided Ukraine with modern weapons such as modern battle tanks. The problem with such advanced systems was the amount of training and maintenance they required. It takes time for four individuals to be trained as a family to operate the American Abrams tank even if the targeting system is easy to use.

Ukraine didn't have time to waste as they sent people who usually operated their Russian T-72 tanks to learn how to operate the Abrams, Challenger, and Leopard tanks. Their initial use of these tanks resulted in defeats. Zelenskyy blamed NATO for sending defective systems.

NATO's response following the missile strike on Poland was to mobilize and send their tanks manned by the crews that knew them the best. In America that was us. We met the Russians on the front within a couple of days of arriving in the country, and we destroyed the Russian tanks, including their latest and greatest, T-14.

After Russia's worst armor defeat, Putin declared we had invaded Russia, as he considered Ukraine a breakaway state that was part of his country. He realized his armor was no match for NATO's best, so he resorted to making his threats come to fruition. He struck NATO's FOBs with tactical nukes. He might have declared the ten to twenty KT tactical weapons 'small,' but history showed that they were the same or larger yield than we used to destroy Hiroshima and Nagasaki. I wonder if anyone felt better telling the Japanese we only used tactical weapons to end the war.

I was away from the FOB when the missiles struck. All of our senior officers had been attending a meeting when the 20KT weapons exploded above our field conference room. The tent material didn't provide any protection against such a weapon.

With the loss of all of in country senior officers I was flocked to the rank of BG. I wore the one-star rank of a BG, but it was only for show. It was decided I needed the rank to pull the division together and without the star the unit colonels wouldn't listen to me.

Of course, we responded to the Russian strike, and as every expert said, the small exchange led to the use of city busting nukes in the hundreds of kiloton range. Hundreds of nukes struck America and hundreds struck Russia.

Upon returning home I'd learned just how bad the Third World War had been. Most of our cities and infrastructure had been destroyed. Washington had been destroyed, with it, the President and Vice President were killed. The Speaker of the House was next in line to become President. He had been on a flight to Washington from California when the balloon went up. His plane crash landed close to Fort Huachuca. He was sworn in as President as soon as his ID was confirmed. It crash-landed because it was a commercial plane, and the EMP from the Russian high-altitude nukes burned out the plane's electric systems. The engines had lost control and had shut themselves down. Orders were waiting for me when I arrived back from Ukraine. I was ordered to meet with the President, who promoted me and asked me to serve as his Secretary of Defense until he could locate a better candidate.

I ran into my best friend, Captain Moore on the ship bringing us home. I promoted him and made him my XO. I knew then he had been exposed to a massive dose of radiation that ate his bone marrow and organs. He developed stage four leukemia and yesterday my best friend and one of the best people I ever knew had peacefully passed in his sleep. When the time comes for me to go, I hope I follow his example. I know I'll see Moore again when I arrive at the gates of Hell. I'm sure most of the people I know will be with me. I don't believe that the last rites will absolve me of the many lives I ordered to be taken or those I took in combat. I'd been told that there was a difference between war and outright murder in the Bible, I really hope so.

I wore my dress uniform for the burial of my best friend. I made sure I wore all of my awards, and I smiled knowing that at least most of mine were won on the battlefield. I don't think I was ever awarded the good conduct ribbon, and if I had, I would have known it was a BS award because I know my record was filled with chicken marks of what I'll call my accomplishments. I laughed thinking of some of them.

My car was waiting to take me to the cemetery. That was the last place I wanted to be. I didn't want to lose my sounding board and friend. He knew me better than I knew myself. I looked at myself in the mirror; was the reflection really me? It looked like an old man wearing a dress uniform. My short hair was white. My face had lines that weren't there six months ago. Stress and a lack of sleep will do that to you. My phone pinged with the message, "It's time."

Time to lay one of the best men I knew to rest. I know he was in pain, and it got to the point where even simple tasks left him breathless. He was too weak to walk from the front door to the rear SCIF. I had gotten him a wheelchair; something he frankly refused to use. He fought up to his last breath. I don't think I could handle the pain he had to endure every day.

It turned out to be wonderful weather that day, no clouds, not even any wind. I wore a pair of dark sunglasses to hide my tear-filled eyes. Moore and I had been friends for over twenty years, and this wasn't the way I thought our friendship would end. I hope he remembers to wait for me before starting the war in Hell. As well as I know him, I'd bet my last dollar he's already trying to figure out how to kill the Devil.

I knew Rand has deep feelings for Captain Gold, he may even be in love with Gold. The least I could do for him was to talk the President into giving him five days to locate her. Rand has been an excellent officer and has excelled at every task he'd been given. Thus, every assignment was tougher than the last. It's that way, the more you succeed, the harder the next mission is. I hope Rand finds Gold alive.

Today I have to lay Moore to rest, and I only hope that Rand doesn't have to do the same with Captain Gold. I thought about transferring her to another unit, but I'm curious how the young Major is going to handle the situation. If he handles it correctly, he's on his way to his stars. Only time will tell.

They're all waiting for me, I wish it was me in that coffin and not Moore, but I guess the Good Lord had other ideas and plans for him. Moore's loss left me with a hole in my TOC. Maybe I should transfer Gold and ask her to assume the position. I wonder what she knows about staff work. I can't afford to pull Rand out of the field.

I picked up a handful of dirt from the pile removed from the grave site. After my short remarks, I tossed the dirt onto the coffin. I also punched his name tag, rank, and rows or awards into the top of the coffin; at least the devil will know who's chasing him. My friend died a hero. I was surprised when I saw President McCarthy with his Secret Service escorts standing in the crowd. He nodded to me. My level of respect for the man just went up one hundred points.

Chapter 3

Rand returned the scout's salute. "Hello Sergeant Bruck. Care to take a little walk with me? I don't usually get the opportunity to go outside and enjoy a little sunshine and fresh air. I have a couple of things I'd like to ask you about."

"Sure thing, Major."

"I'd like to figure out how you managed to travel from Captain Gold's FOB to here without seeing any trace of the Warlord's troops. Did you at least manage to send the correct code to Captain Gold?"

"Major, of course I did."

Rand pulled a small notebook from his blouse pocket. "Just so we're on the same page, what was the letter group you sent?"

"Sir, I know the daily code!"

"Excellent. What were the letters you sent to Captain Gold?"

"I personally sent the code. I checked the daily codes for the 14th."

"Sergeant today is the 13th. You sent the code yesterday, didn't you?"

"Yes, Sir."

"Then you sent the wrong code. Can't you read? Do you have any idea how a daily code book works?"

"Major, of course I do."

"I think not. You mixed up the dates. What was the code you sent?"

"Let me have a minute. I remember now, it was OQ."

"OQ? Sergeant, what is wrong with you? That's not even the code for the 14th. I think you're on the Warlord's payroll. I think you intentionally screwed up."

Sergeant Bruck broke out sweating, as Rand waved Sergeant Reynolds over. "Sergeant Reynolds, I believe we have one of the Warlord's people with us. I suggest you place him under arrest and ask the nice MPs if they can think of a way to force the truth from his lying tongue."

Reynolds smiled. "Yes, sir. I believe they have a new drug they've been dying to use. I understand it forces the suspect to answer every question."

Rand smiled. "That sounds wonderful. Are there any side effects?"

"Yes, sir. The person is never the same again. Their brain is fried like they had a serious stroke."

"Is it reversible?"

"Sir, they told me it wasn't. The person ends up like a well-cooked vegetable."

Rand smiled and looked at Bruck. "Oh well, I guess it's worth it to get to the truth. Sergeant Bruck, I'm sorry in advance if you were actually telling me the truth and you have to spend the rest of your life as a vegetable."

Bruck screamed, "You can't do that. I demand a court..."

"Didn't you hear that we're under a state of national martial law? There are no courts. I may never see you again, and even if I did, you wouldn't recognize me or even know where you were." Rand nodded to Reynolds. "Take him away and have the transcript brought to me when they're finished with him." Rand smiled, and it came out more like a leer. "You screwed up big time and you are going to pay the price for your incompetence."

Bruck screamed and begged for mercy as he was dragged away to a fate worse than death. Rand shook his head. *OQ? Where the hell did that come from? It's not even in the code book. Is it one of the Warlord's codes? I knew Bruck was dumb, but I really didn't believe he was a spy, not until I looked into his eyes, and he told me the two-letter code he'd sent to Captain Gold. I wonder what happened to her convoy and where Karen is? Shit, if anything happened to her, I'll go crazy. I finally found someone I really care about and what happens? They put her in my TOC so I can't touch her and then she disappears along with her entire convoy.*

Rand walked to the motor pool to check on the vehicles in case he needed to get a rescue mission together, when he was interrupted by an unknown man who looked homeless. Rand was about to call security when the stranger held up a set of dog tags. "Major, I'm Master Sergeant David Crockett, I lead the Delta detachment you were told to expect."

"Master Sergeant, welcome. Is that your real name? Should I assume you carry a Bowie knife on your belt? Did you just come from the Alamo?"

"Major, it's my name for this mission. I've had so many it's hard to remember the name my parents gave me."

"In that case, welcome. Please follow me to the SCIF so we can discuss the details of your mission."

"Sir, I was briefed on our way here. I brought a team of twenty-four battle-tested people who are experts at hostage rescue. Major, if she's alive, we'll find her."

Rand stopped walking. "And if she's not alive?"

Crockett smiled. "Major, in that case, we'll kill everyone we find, and we'll dig them out of any nests they're hiding in. We'll capture a few to question, and I can tell you, they will break. Speaking of which, I have orders to take your prisoner, Sergeant Bruck. My people will break him within two hours, and we won't leave him brain dead, which is what the truth serum would have done to him."

"Master Sergeant, he's all yours. I never want to see him again."

"Sir, you won't. I can promise you that I'm not very big on second chances when the person attempts to harm or bring possible harm to people I like, and so far, you are all at the top of the good list."

"Excellent, Master Sergeant. How do your drugs compare to our new ones?"

"Night and day. Our techs will know everything he knows within thirty minutes. While we wait, do you happen to have any cold beer at your little hacienda?"

"Mr. Crockett, of course we do."

"Major, Just David or Master Sergeant will be fine."

"Master Sergeant, do you have any idea where they might be keeping the hostages? In your experience, do you think there's a chance Captain Gold is still alive?"

Crockett spit a wad of chewing tobacco on the dry ground and pushed it around with his boot before he looked at Rand. "Major, I read the file. I know you two were attracted to each other, and I know you want to go with us or send your own people to tear every square inch of the area between us and where the drone saw some trucks. If she's alive, and I believe she is, we'll find her."

Rand felt a knot growing in his stomach. "Master Sergeant, why do you think they're keeping her alive?"

"Because they don't know what the OQ code means, and since the sergeant screwed up and sent a two-letter code that doesn't exist, and they don't know he screwed up, they're most likely trying to break her. And when they do, they'll learn, if they don't already know, about the two of you. Then she becomes very valuable. She's ransom material to get whatever they want from you."

"How would they know about the two of us?"

"Major, you're not dealing with a typical nut case. She is smart and was trained the same way both of you were. She is very dangerous. Of the fifty or so Warlords operating in the country, she's the most dangerous."

Rand stopped walking. "Fifty Warlords?"

"At last count. There used to be sixty-one, but my team has been very busy. If you don't mind, I'd like my specialist to have a little chat with Sergeant Bruck."

"Master Sergeant, he's all yours. Will you be keeping me in the loop of your investigation?"

"You'll get a copy of my report when we complete our mission."

Rand stopped at the door to the prison. Two MPs armed with M4s and M17 sidearms snapped to attention when Rand approached them. "Master Sergeant, what exactly is your mission?"

"Major, our mission, like yours, is to make America safe again. You might say, we're like garbage men who show up to take out the trash. We locate the trash, we process the trash, and we make sure the trash is properly disposed of."

Crockett smiled and spat another mouthful of tobacco juice on the ground. This time it landed inches from Rand's right boot.

Rand knew Crockett was trying to push his buttons, so he ignored it. "Sergeant, please find the captain. I need either her returned, or closure... and I like revenge very much."

"Major, we're both playing from the same book. My team and I live for revenge. With all due respect, we'd like to get started."

"Sergeant, may God protect you."

"Major, thank you. I put my faith in the Good Lord, my vest, and my M7."

Rand saluted the MPs, and then he returned to his office. He was a third of the way back when he heard a blood-chilling scream coming from the prison. He stopped to listen, wanting to make sure the sound he'd heard was a scream and not the wind.

Rand nodded his head. *Yup, that was a scream. Whatever they did to Bruck, he deserves it. He most likely let the convoy roll into an ambush. Had he been doing his job, the convoy might have been prepared and turned the ambush around, so the Warlord's people were the ones being shot. If his neglect led to Karen's harm, I'll personally tear him apart with my own two hands.*

Master Sergeant Crockett smiled as he watched Sergeant Bruck scream. He'd been injected with a new drug. When he lied, the drug caused him enormous pain. He felt like his entire body was on fire. The pain continued for five minutes; those minutes felt like an eternity to Bruck. As soon as the pain wore off the next question was asked, and if Bruck lied the pain started again. Once Bruck learned by telling the truth, or what he believed was the truth, the pain stopped. He admitted to being high and that's how he had mixed up the code.

Crockett couldn't decide if Bruck was a spy or if he was just stupid. He decided on the sergeant being just stupid for now and planned to take him with them, thinking that if he made one move to give their position away, he promised he'd put a bullet in Bruck's head.

Ninety minutes after arriving, Crockett led his people toward where the drone had picked up the abandoned trucks. They traveled in what appeared to be thirty-year-old pickups. What appeared to be surface rust was actually painted and clear-coated to look like rust. Their chassis and engines had been rebuilt to allow the pickups the power of a supercar. Anyone seeing the trucks would think they weren't anything other than old rust buckets that had survived the war because they didn't have any electronics to be burned out. The glass had been replaced with bullet-resistant crystal.

The trucks' body panels were lined with Kevlar and ceramic armor that could stop anything up to a 50-caliber bullet. The fuel tanks and tires were self-sealing. The engine hoses were wrapped in steel pipes. The engine compartments were lined with ceramic armor similar to what was applied to the American M1A3 main battle tanks. The bumpers were heavy steel, designed to push other vehicles off the road. Crockett knew he was up against overwhelming numbers, so they had to use every trick in their book to succeed in the mission. Heavy machine guns were stored in the pickup's beds. They could be installed in seconds turning the trucks into what was named technicals.

None of the Delta Detachment had shaved in days, most hadn't bathed in three days, and all wore dirty clothes over their vests. All wore oversized clothes, so they looked like everyone else in America: hungry and destitute.

Their new M7 assault rifles were chambered in the new 6.8 mm rounds that could defeat any known body armor, were in hidden components in the trucks. They carried a sidearm of their choice under their baggy clothes and all had at least two hidden small guns on them as well as at least two fighting knives. Delta were the best at what they did, and after the brief nuclear war with Russia, they were used putting down insurrections and killing Warlords. Today was just another day at the office for them.

The Delta convoy looked like any other militia, they flew bright yellow

Gadsden flags that proudly showed the snake and its message of 'Don't Tread On me.' Sharon's scouts saw the approaching convoy, and they noted the out-of-tune sound of the engines, but they didn't realize they were listening to a recording. They nodded to themselves when the rust was reflected in the setting sun, and the bright yellow flags pushed them over the edge. The scouts called their Warlord. "Ma'am, a small group of trucks is approaching our first roadblock."

Letts grabbed the mic, "What do they look like?"

The lead scout laughed. "Ma'am, they look like us: dirty and hungry."

"Okay, you can approach. Just make sure this isn't some kind of trick."

"Ma'am, has the Army ever looked like us? Wouldn't they be well-fed? They're not in uniforms. I thought the military wasn't allowed to fly our flag."

"Wait, did you just say they were flying our flag?"

"Yes, Ma'am. Bright yellow flying in the wind."

"Stop them and report what you find. If the hairs on the back of your head feel funny, kill them. I don't want to take any chances."

Chapter 4

Crockett's driver, Corporal Edwards said, "We're being watched. The hills are alive with assholes. The thermal sensors are showing them trying to hide behind the coverage on both sides of the road."

"Good, let them watch. I don't think they have anything that can hurt us..."

"What about what they stole or were given from the armories?"

"Yeah, but we have a few tricks up our sleeves too. Tell me if the thermals pick up any launches or shooting."

"You got it. Please don't tell me you're going to take a nap. You know that every time you've ever taken a nap we've ended up in the shit."

"You don't really believe those stories, do you?"

"What stories? I was on those missions with you. I drove for Master Sergeant Dillon before he bought the farm. I want you to know I don't like large animals and I have no interest in living on a farm so don't make me pay for one."

Crockett smiled; his people always knew when to break the ice with a short joke. "They're watching us while we watch them. Hopefully, they'll see our flags and think we're a local militia come to join up with them. Of course, if they don't buy it then we'll have to kill most of them until we find one who can tell us where Captain Gold and their Warlord is. I'd loved to have a double: return the captain alive and make sure the Warlord is dead. I really hate Warlords."

"I hope you're right, because based on the asses on the hills I'd say we're outnumbered five or more to one."

"That's our normal odds... just another day in paradise. I wish someone would really care to send us their best and outnumber us ten to one so we can put a stop to these assholes who want to play God. I'd like a nice fight once in a while. All we get is the order to slaughter people who should know better. Oh well, another day, another bloodbath. Inform everyone to be ready. Are the miniguns ready?"

"They show green, armed, and are slaved to our thermal sensors. They aren't in their firing position. Do you want to power them up and rise them above the bed?"

"Not yet, there's no reason to show them our toys. Just send the signal to power them and place them in hot stand by."

"Sir, done. All trucks signal they're ready. The thermals sensors are marking the tangos' locations. I've had their positions to the fire control computer."

Crockett nodded. "The assholes can't hide their body temperature from thermal sensors. When the times to hit them, we'll be very happy the miniguns and machine guns were rechambled for the new 6.8 rounds that will make them into chopped meat.

"Good, but if we take this Sharon Letts down that will leave us with what exactly, 49 other Warlords to take her place? Power hates a vacuum, and what if these people with a little training or just the guns decided to control their local areas? This one is unusual in that, according to the reports, she controls what's left of four states. She ain't going to control shit in about thirty seconds though."

The driver said, "Boss, looks like we've got a welcoming committee up ahead. They have a nice little roadblock of cars. The drone doesn't see any Jersey Walls, just the cars. And according to the temperature, we have at least fifteen people waiting to welcome us."

"Well, then, I guess we should give them a warm welcome of our own. I hate wasting time and words." Crockett checked the feed from the drone and nodded to himself. "Alert everyone, we're going hot in twenty, fifteen, ten, five... three, two, one, weapons are green, repeat, all weapons are hot. Free at will."

The driver smiled. "Who's Will?"

"Shut up and open fire. The sooner we break through their roadblock and terminate their people in the hills, the sooner we'll find the captain. Make sure we have at least one captive alive to question."

"Boss, you take all of the fun out of it. "The miniguns jumped into their firing positions and began pouring copper and lead into Letts' people. "Sergeant, we're firing. The body count is going down like..."

"Don't say it."

The seven-barrel mini-guns rose from their protected cases and opened fire at their assigned targets. Each gun could fire three thousand rounds a minute. The first and second rounds fired were armor piercing, the third and fifth were JHP and the fourth round was a tracer. Anyone seeing the firing would think they were seeing a laser firing. The firing until the large six-thousand-round ammo boxes were empty.

When the ammo cans were empty, a crew member had to replace them with a new one. The trucks carried three spare ammo boxes. Crockett's driver had closed the blast shields that covered the truck's windows. He drove by the image of the grill-mounted camera that projected its view onto the inside of the windshield. "Boss, RPGs!"

"Real RPGs or the LAWs they most likely stole from the Guard's armory?"

"LAWs, one shot and toss it. They're old but can do a lot of damage to us."

"Pop the chaff, they might be able to confuse the incoming. Sometimes the rockets strike the chaff and explode away from us. It's a long shot but it's the only one we have."

The driver shook his head. "Not if we can rush into the middle of the assholes behind the roadblock. The miniguns tore through the cars. We shredded them so we should have no problem driving through the debris."

"Then do it and hurry before one of those assholes realizes he has to aim the damn rocket."

The LAWs rockets were unguided because they were designed as a short-range weapon that a soldier could use against armored vehicles. Their HEAT warheads would easily burn through the sheet metal and the thin layer of ceramic armor applied to the Delta's doors. They would have destroyed the trucks had they connected with them, but when they were fired, the trucks moved, and only one managed to connect with its target, impacting the large bumper. The rocket tore the bumper off of the truck, and the truck drove over the smoking bumper and then followed Crockett's first truck through the remains of the cars that had formed the roadblock.

Delta's trucks, then the miniguns, poured thousands of bullets into the surrounding hills guided by thermal sensors. Letts' troops thought they had cover, but what they really had was concealment. The bushes and trees offered no real cover at all, and the new 6.8 mm rounds easily tore through trees, brushes, and earthen walls. Thousands of armor-piercing rounds tore apart anyone they connected with.

Letts had anticipated the use of miniguns, and she had ordered her people to hide deep in their foxholes until the guns ran out of ammunition, leaving a window when the Delta troops had to switch the ammo boxes that fed the guns. It was at this moment that Letts' troops made a mass charge against the Delta troops and their vehicles.

Hundreds of angry, heavily-armed men and women, mostly carrying automatic M4s that they'd stolen from National Guard armories, poured out of their foxholes like red ants that had their nest upset. Many fired from the hip, hoping their rounds would prevent the Delta troops from being able to reload the miniguns. The upside of the minigun was its ability to pour thousands of rounds at an unbelievable speed, but the downside was that the six-hundred-round boxes weighed more than one man could carry since they had to carry the ammo and the 28-volt batteries that powered them. It took a four-man crew to change the ammo on the gun, and it also took them the better part of ten minutes to slide a full magazine that linked to the large and heavy auto minigun. The operators then had to install a new ammo box that weighed a few hundred pounds, they had to reconnect the battery to the gun.

They didn't have ten minutes, as rounds began to impact too close for comfort. Crockett told the team to have three of them work on the reloading while the fourth member of each truck returned fire with their new M7 rifles. The new 6.8 mm rounds had no trouble penetrating the vests stolen from the armories. Crocker smiled seeing the rounds knocking attackers down left, right, and center. He mentally counted the numbers, *shit, there's just too many of them. We'll have to switch to the heavier shit.*

Crockett ordered the 60 mm mortars fired. "Fry them! Use the WP shells mixed with smoke."

Staff Sergeant Brill asked, "Master Sergeant, smoke?"

"Yes, smoke to cover us. The quicker we can get the miniguns reloaded, the sooner we can kill them. The smoke should make it hard for them to see us, our thermal sensors will allow us to see and target them. Remember, we're on a mission from God. We've been ordered to clean the gene pool, and we're going to make sure these assholes don't breed. So yes, smoke and WP. The WP will scare the crap out of them while the dense smoke hides us from them."

A moment later, Crockett smiled as he heard the familiar thump, thump sound of the small mortar rounds being fired. The mortar teams stayed under the line of sight. They reached to the mortar tubes to drop new rounds down the tube, the rounds landed on the firing pin that ignited the charge that ignited the powered fuel to ignite.

Crockett watched them impact on the hillsides. The WP burned everything it touched, while the smoke rounds bloomed into thick gray smoke that burned the eyes and lungs. The attackers stopped running. Many dropped their rifles and were bent over coughing. Mucus poured from their noses, and they rubbed their burning eyes. Some got turned around and ran back up the hills only to be caught under the blooming clouds of the WP launched by the mortars.

Shards of the burning metal landed on Letts' people. The WP burned through the skin and even through bones. The screams that echoed between the two hills sounded like the sound effects from a bad horror movie.

The smoke and WP stopped the attackers in their tracks, as Letts watched the events unfold from a drone that flew circles overhead. She was about to issue new orders when the video from her drone stopped. She looked at the drone controller angrily. "Did they shoot it down?"

"Yes, Ma'am. It's gone. I've got no signals from it."

"Do you have another ready to launch?"

"Ma'am, I do but they're now alerted to our drones so any we send up will most likely be shot down before it even reaches the hills."

"Without them I'm blind, and if I'm blind, I can't issue orders to our people. Would you like them to be slaughtered? If they are, then there won't be anyone standing between us, YOU, and those troops. I have to hand it to them they are very well trained. Compared to the captain's troops, these must be their A team because they move like they've done this a hundred times before."

The drone tech responded, "Ma'am, Rangers?"

"Maybe, but I took the Ranger course and even after the war they wouldn't let them run around looking like that. I'd bet on SEALs or maybe even a surviving CIA action group."

The tech shook his head. "I didn't think any of the CIA action groups remained."

"Neither did I, but these people move like a well-oiled machine. Pack up your equipment and let's move to our alternative headquarters."

The commander of her personal protection detail asked, "Ma'am, what about the captain? Should I dispose of her?"

Letts shook her head. "No imagination. We're taking her with us. Make sure she's drugged and blindfolded. We can't take any chances with her seeing where we're going."

"I'll make sure the doc knocks her out and she stays out for the duration of our move. Cover her face so their damn eyes in the sky may see us loading someone into the trucks, they won't be able to make out who it is. Make sure she's comfortable when we reach base station beta. Lock her in one of the special guest suites and place a guard in front of her door; someone very trustworthy. Remember her value to us is decreased if she's harmed."

Her executive officer nodded and replied, "I have already issued the orders to prepare her for travel and to knock her out and place her in a body bag."

"Excellent thinking. This battle is finished. Issue the recall for any of the survivors. Any who are too burned or can't keep up should be sent to facility number five."

"Ma'am, number five? That's the..."

"I know what it is! I had it built. Now follow my orders or you can accompany them."

The major swallowed, realizing how close he'd come to being a patient at facility number five. Five was famous, as the people who entered never usually exited. Those who did manage to leave were never the same. The life behind their eyes was gone. They screamed most of the night, and their days were consumed with pain and memories of horrible acts that had been done to them. The facility had been the idea of an indicted doctor who had been charged with sexually harassing his patients. He liked to inflict pain on others, sometimes, even his patients. It's a god thing we found him before their army did. They would have arrested him and likely killed him. His lucky day was when found him. He must have thought the world had ended. He was torturing to death everyone who landed in his labs."

There were rumors that two of the doctor's neighbors who had played their music too loud had been kidnapped by the doctor and that he had taken his time torturing them in his basement.

The war had saved him from a trial, as the press had said he was either going to take a plea deal or he was going to prison for twenty to thirty years. The doctor had assumed the name of Doctor Strange and strange he was. He wasn't interested in healing; he just wanted to see how much pain his patients could endure. Letts placed him in charge of interrogation. Even a whisper of being sent to facility 5 would drastically improve someone's performance. It was rumored that the doctor was insane. It was also rumored the United States had a bounty of ten thousand dollars in gold for information leading to his arrest. Letts knew none of her people would attempt to cash in on the information, though, because if they got caught, they would be looking at an endless amount of pain and suffering.

Crockett watched Letts' people withdraw, and he ordered his team to launch a high-flying stealth drone to find and follow her, destroy her network, arrest or kill her, and save the captain. Crockett considered all of the above to be the only satisfying way their meeting could end.

Rand received the raw video feed from the drone he was flying above the battle. He had to admit Crockett led a well-trained and lethal platoon. He felt a glimmer of hope that he might actually be able to save Gold. Rand couldn't view the images from the drone Crockett had launched.

Chapter 5

I needed a new executive officer. My staff knew not to remind me because it was like opening a festering wound. I had not buried my best friend. He died because we were full of our own BS. We thought that the Russians would never release the 'genie' from its bottle again. It was okay for us to give birth to the 'genie' and let him loose twice over Japan. The thought at the time was that they deserved it. They'd attacked us without warning or a declaration of war.

A pre-declaration of war always sounded to me like saying, 'Let's have a war. Does Sunday morning on December 7th suit you? If so, please consider us at war and we'll see you at dawn.'

What a complete load of BS. Putin had promised to stop NATO from invading what he considered to be part of Russia. I wonder how we would have responded if Russian troops had invaded Alaska or maybe California. I laughed to myself, Yeah, they could have had California, and we would have most likely given it to them as long as they promised not to give it back to us. California, the land of 'fruits and nuts.' They were blessed with perfect weather and hundreds of miles of beautiful beaches, and what did they do with their blessings? They destroyed paradise, with some help from the Russians of course. San Diego, LA, San Fransico, Oakland, Sacramento, Long Beach, Bakersfield, Riverside, and San Jose were incinerated in the Russian attack.

I never understood why they nuked Riverside; the SAC base there had been closed for years. I think some of the Russian missile batteries never updated their targets. It doesn't matter now, what's done is done. Most of California won't be able to support life for a generation or three. The Russians used ground bursts to generate massive fallout clouds and the crazies placed massive nuclear mines along the west coast. Thank you God for stopping all but the one located at the LA harbor. That one nuclear mine threw dirty water vapor into the atmosphere, knowing full well the winds blew west to east, seeding the winds with fallout. What they didn't count on was that the nuclear explosions had altered the Jet Stream.

Instead of dusting the breadbasket with deadly fallout, our northern neighbor received the bulk of the deadly gift. They weren't prepared for it. In the course of a couple of weeks, they lost seventy percent of their population.

Of course, millions were killed when Toronto, Ottawa, Victoria, and Montreal received nuclear strikes. Calgary became the new capital of Canada; they begged us for assistance, something we didn't have any of to spare. When their new government realized, we weren't coming to their aid, they threw us a curve ball, they turned around and said if we weren't going to send them aid, they then asked to join us. Their Prime Minister said he would dissolve Canada and would resign if we would accept them into the Union.

The President asked me my thoughts on accepting them into America. I told him that on one hand, it was the right thing to do, but on the other, we couldn't even care for our own people. That's when he reminded me that we were weeks behind in our plan to relocate the government. I accepted his criticism and offered to resign. He tore up my resignation letter and told me I wasn't getting out of it that easy. He was sorry for the loss of Colonel Moore, but he wasn't going to release me. He told me that he liked and trusted me. I reminded him that I was a major just a few months ago. He laughed and told me if I wasn't careful, he'd stick another star on my shoulders just to piss me off. I got the message, and I placed a call to Major Rand.

One thing I learned very early in my career was that shit flowed downhill, and being a LTG, my shit was about to fall on a certain major who was behind schedule. Nothing a little motivational chat couldn't solve. I'll warn him that if he doesn't get his ass to Kansas City then I'm going to make him my XO. The President had given him five days, he'd even sent him a squad of Deltas to locate Captain Gold, it was time to hit the road.

When Rand disconnected his call with the SecDoD, his face had lost all color. He cursed in three languages then called his staff together so he could teach them what happens when the shit flowed down. He gave orders to break camp at dawn, and he ordered the scouts to be on the road by 0400 and to report every thirty minutes.

Rand's S2 asked, "Sir, what about Davy Crockett?"

The S4 looked confused. "Didn't he already die at the Alamo?"

Rand was in no mood for jokes after just having had his ass chewed. He looked at his staff menacingly and said, "Listen up, there will be no more BS about Master Sergeant Davy Crockett. I don't believe for a minute that that's his real name, but he's the one who's leading the Delta Detachment to locate Captain Gold. Even if he isn't letting us know his real name, the SecDoD has placed his trust in the Master Sergeant, and so will we. As much as I want us to locate and free Captain Gold, the SecDoD has reminded me in plain language that we have a mission to accomplish for the President, and he's getting very antsy that we're behind schedule. Therefore, we are out of here at 0500. That gives the scouts an hour ahead of us to make sure we don't run into any ambushes like Gold's convoy did."

The S2 asked, "Sir, so you believe her convoy ran into one of Letts' famous traps?"

"I do. I also believe the man we're holding in our brig is responsible. Master Sergeant Crockett believes he's outright dumb and missed the signs of the ambush because he was high. I don't believe it. I still believe he's playing for the other side and as such, he's staying locked up. He's not going to make any calls or see anyone except for the Master Sergeant. If something happens to Crockett, then someone is going to be very lonely, spending the rest of his life in the deepest hole I can drop him in."

The head of his protection detail said, "Sir, I can make that happen right now; just say the word. If he's the reason, we lost the captain's convoy then I'll take pleasure in putting him in a box."

"LT, maybe after the Master Sergeant returns, if he doesn't meet up with us by the time we reach Kansas City, then I'll return here do it myself. I'm leaving a squad to turn this into a walled FOB. With all of these warlords running around crazy. The locals are going to need more help than their small police departments can accomplish."

The LT shook his head. "Sir don't dirty your hands. If you deem it has to be done in order to save lives, then I'd be happy to carry out your order."

"Thank you. I'll let you know. For now, detail three of your people to guard him." Rand looked around the crowded room. "Does anyone have anything else to ask?"

When no one did, Rand nodded. "Ladies and gentlemen, we are wheels up at 0500 and not a minute later. Prepare your people and let's hit the road."

When Rand was alone, he silently moved to the center of his tent. He stood under the peak, with the only light coming from a small white candle. He got on his knees and prayed for the safe return of Captain Gold, offering his life in exchange for hers.

*****

Captain Gold dreamed she was with Rand on a white sandy beach. There were rows of multi-colored umbrellas, each with a matching large towel and two beach chairs under them. She walked to the water's edge, not understanding why the only thing she heard was the crashing of the waves against the beach.

The next instant she saw she was walking along the beach until she saw two large letters, OQ, formed from the sand. The two letters towered over her. She stopped in front of the sand sculpture. She didn't understand why anyone would spend the time making a sculpture of two letters that didn't belong together. She couldn't remember if she'd ever heard of them being together.

The wind around her echoed the letters "OQ, OQ," but she didn't understand the word, only the letters. She walked into the warm water until it was up to her neck. Once she was in the water, she couldn't remember why she'd walked into the ocean.

She saw the two letters floating past her on the waves. She scanned her memory and couldn't figure out the meaning of the two letters. Letts watched the monitors showing Gold's state of mind and body. She couldn't understand why the captain hadn't broken and told her what the code meant. Letts said to her medical tech, "If we can't break her then we can still find a use for her. Use the drug to screw with her memory, and embed a tracking pellet in her so we can see where they take her. We'll drop her off out front where that squad is searching, and if we're lucky they'll take her to their FOB, and we'll know where to strike."

"Ma'am, if we hit her memory, there's a ninety percent chance she won't recover it."

"What do I care if she remembers her first kiss or screw? I don't want her remembering anything about her captivity."

"Yes, ma'am. I'll prepare the injection."

Crockett's radio beeped. He was angry that his newbie had called again. This would make it the fourth time this morning. Crockett shook his head, *damn war, we were so short of people that we put the normal selection process on hold and what do I get? A Ranger who can't think for himself.* "Benson, what is it this time? Are you lost?"

"Master Sergeant, I found her."

"Who her?"

"Captain Gold."

"Ping me your location. I'll be right there. Does she need the doc?"

"I don't know. She doesn't seem to remember anything, not even who she is."

"Shit. Listen to me. Don't report her find to HQ. Leave that to me. And whatever you do, don't lose her. Put her in your HUMVEE and don't let her out. Do you understand me?"

"Yes. I'll lock her in the HUMVEE. I think you should bring a spare uniform."

"Please tell me she's not wandering around naked."

"She's in a hospital gown."

"Shit. I'll be at your location in four minutes."

Rand was overjoyed that they'd located Captain Gold. He didn't know yet that she wasn't aware of who she was or where she had been. She kept looking at the sky saying how pretty it looked. Benson gave his location to Crockett, who said to Staff Sergeant Brinks, "Something stinks in the way Benson found her. He said she was walking along the freeway with no idea who she was or where she was going. My gut is screaming at me that she's the bait for an ambush."

Staff Sergeant Brinks replied, "What makes you think that?"

Crockett got angry. "Don't you find it a little unusual that we're looking for her, and all of sudden, she shows up in a hospital gown with no memory? There's no working hospital within one hundred miles of our position. The only logical answer is that Letts had her, and then she released her, so we'd find her. I don't know why, but I'm going to get to the bottom of this. Has she said anything?"

"She repeats that her name is Captain, and she looks and acts confused when we ask her how she managed to find us or where she'd been."

"She said her name was Captain?"

"I showed her, her dog tags. She acted as if she had no idea what they were. When I told her that her name was Karen Gold, she told me her name was Captain. I read the first four numbers of her social security number from her dog tags and asked her to finish the number. She didn't understand what a number was."

"Shit. Someone, and I think we know who, screwed up her memory; unless of course, she had a stroke and she really can't remember anything, but I doubt it.

Scan her for explosives. They have turned her into a living IED."

"Will do. Master Sergeant, why does she think her name is Captain?"

"It's most likely what they called her. It's the only name she remembers. We need to get her to a hospital that has a CT scanner so they can look at the damage to her mind. I wouldn't want to be in Letts' shoes when Major Rand finds out his girlfriend is damaged goods."

Chapter 6

Rand's scouts stopped on I-44 before they reached the tunnel ahead of the I-64 loop around Tulsa. They'd been warned to avoid Tulsa proper due to it having been struck by the Russians and the reported violent gang activity. The scouts' leader, LT Bill Maynard, made them stop before they reached any potential ambush sites, places he would have set up an ambush if he wanted to kill anyone trying to avoid the city.

Maynard sent two men to recon the tunnel, and they returned with shocking information. "Sir, the entrance to the tunnel is blocked with an old police car and a school bus."

Maynard said, "When you say old, can you place a year on what you saw?"

Private Scot shook his head. "Sir, I can't, but I can draw it."

"Show me."

Private Scot drew a picture of the police car he saw. Maynard smiled. "That's pretty good. Did you take art classes?"

"Yes, sir. I wanted to be an artist, but they don't earn shit, so I went into digital art where I could design games."

"For your information, what you saw was a late fifties car. It didn't have anything that could be burned out by the nuke EMP. I bet it still runs, same as the school bus. I bet they were in someone's collection and used for parades or whatever. What matters though is that the mouth of the tunnel is blocked. Did you see any people behind or in the car and bus?"

"Sir, we saw four people with ARs and two with bolt action hunting rifles."

"Great. Just great. I don't want to get into a firefight with our own citizens. What else did you see?"

"There is power and light in the tunnel."

"How?"

"I didn't get close enough to see. I could see the light reflecting from the windows in the school bus."

Corporal Milner spoke up for the first time. "I wonder if they used the tunnels as shelters when the warning came?"

Maynard shook his head. "Corporal, there wasn't a warning."

Milner looked shocked. "Sir, what do you mean there wasn't a warning? Surely a warning would have saved millions."

"As far as I understand, they felt that a warning would cause mass panic. People wouldn't be able to escape the cities, so they would have been tied up in bumper-to-bumper traffic and thus trapped when the missiles arrived. Since the Russians struck at night, those in power decided it was better to let the population sleep. They didn't even warn where the fallout would fall. I don't know what would be better, to have a warning and take their chances, escaping from the cities or dying in their sleep. I think I would have chosen to go in my sleep. One moment sleeping and the next standing in front of the Lord."

Milner asked, "Then why the people in the tunnels?"

"Someone must have been able to plot the fallout and get as many people as they could to shelter in the tunnels. The map shows two. Did you get a chance to check out the second one?"

"No, sir. We couldn't reach it over the mountains, and we returned at the time you ordered us to report to you. Sir, the second tunnel is after the loop that takes us around the city. Sir, what are your orders?"

"I want the two of you to change out of your uniforms and put on your dirtiest pair of jeans and shirts. Rub some dirt on your exposed skin and carry one of the bolt action rifles and a shotgun so you look like a couple of survivors attempting to reach family in Kansas City. Ask for permission to pass through the tunnel. Keep your small radios on so I can follow whatever they say to you. If you run into trouble, we'll have your six."

"You want us to be spies?"

"I want you to SCOUT and get us the information we need in order to figure out what I should do. Now go change and show me how you look before you leave."

Milner asked, "How are we supposed to get to the tunnel? We can't use one of our vehicles."

"The good Lord gave you two legs and two feet, so walk. You should be covered in sweat by the time you reach the tunnel. It will help make you look like a couple of survivors. Decide beforehand where the two of are from and where in Kansas City you're going. Here's a spare paper map. I've marked your path in yellow, so you can show this to whoever stops you. It should convince them you're real."

Milner and Scot were covered in dust and sweat when they approached the roadblock at the entrance to the tunnel. "Stop where you are! Drop your weapons! All of them on the ground now. Take two steps forward and place your hands behind your heads. If you move, you'll die. You're covered by at least five guns. If we find any weapons on you when we search you, we will kill you, so drop any that you have, and that includes knives."

Milner and Scot dropped their rifles, knives, and two small semi-automatic pistols, then they placed their hands behind their heads and stood still while four men, two of whom were armed with M4s, approached them. The one wearing a gold sheriff star asked, "Who are you and what are you doing here?"

Milner slowly responded, "We're trying to reach some of our relatives who live outside of Kansas City. We started out from Fort Worth, and it's taken us nine weeks to get here. We started with a 64 Chevy that was stolen from us fifty miles ago. We walked the rest of the way. All we want is your permission to cross through your tunnel so we can pick up the loop around Tulsa and continue with our trek."

The sheriff stared at the two men standing in front of him. "Show me the bottom of your boots."

Scott knew they'd been busted. "Sherrif, I can't lift my legs. It's old back injury from when I played HS football."

The Sherrif smiled. "No problem." He looked at his deputies. "Pull their boots off their feet."

"Look at these. I believe these are US military boots. Are you boys' deserters? We support our military and don't take kindly to deserters. I don't believe your story."

"We're not deserters. We bought these boots at an Army-Navy store before the war. We thought they would be good for when we went hunting."

The Sheriff shook his head. "What were you hunting?"

"Deer and wild pigs."

"What type of rifles did you use and name the ammo."

"Remington 700 chambered in 308."

The Sheriff didn't know what to make of them. "I have a problem. I don't know if I believe you or not. I have a hunch that your trouble, but I don't know why. Like maybe you're scouts for a larger force that wants what we have. Maybe you want the tunnel for yourselves. But then again, maybe you are who you say you are. I need to chat with a couple of the elders who run this facility."

Scott looked surprised. "You call the tunnel a facility?"

"Yes. It has provided shelter and a home for many people who no longer have one thanks to the fallout. There are families here, women and children. If you so much as harm a single hair on any of their heads, I'll have you skinned alive, and I'll enjoy hearing you scream. Do you understand me?"

Milner nodded his head. "Yes, sir. We do. We only want to pass through your tunnel."

"I'll have people watching you. We'll return your weapons when you're one hundred yards from the other side."

Scott asked, "Do you know anything about the next tunnel?"

The Sheriff looked into Scott's eyes. "Now why would you want to know about the other tunnel when the loop you said you want is between the two? Maybe my gut was right and you're not who you say you are." He nodded to the two men standing next to him. "Handcuff them. Something isn't right and we're going to get to the bottom of it. Take the one with the big mouth first. You know what to do. It always loosens their tongues."

Scott was dragged into what had been a maintenance room and strapped to a folding table. One of the men leered at him. "Did you ever read the book 1984?"

Scott's voice broke in fear. "No, why?"

"They had a brilliant way of getting to the truth."

"Drugs? I like drugs."

The deputy laughed. "Not drugs. Something much more effective."

A woman carried a small cage into the room and looked at Scott tied to the table. "Do you know what's in the cage?"

Scott shook his head and she laughed. "I can't hear you."

"No, I have no idea what's in the cage."

"It's a rat. A big fu-king rat, and a very hungry one at that. We're going to rub some bacon grease on your stomach and hold the cage over you. My little friend here is going to begin eating through your skin. It usually only takes a couple of minutes to get to the truth. Are you ready? My little friend is hungry, and you look like you haven't missed any meals; not like the rest of us."

Scott screamed, "You wouldn't! You can't. There are laws against torture."

"Who said anything about torture? I assure you my little pet isn't going to be tortured."

She rubbed bacon grease on Scott's skin, and as soon as the rat smelled it, it began running around in circles inside its cage. She looked at Scott who was terrified and began screaming, "You can't do this! It's not right."

"Now just lay there and be a nice snack to my little pet."

Scott screamed as the cage was placed on his stomach. She just smiled and said, "Don't move. I'll just pull the bottom tray out and my little pet here will begin feasting on you."

"I'll talk! I'll tell you anything you want to know."

She looked at the deputy who said, "Place the cage on him, but don't pull the bottom tray until we hear what he has to say." The deputy smiled at Scott. "Your turn to talk, and if I was in your shoes, I'd tell us the truth and say it very quickly or her pet gets a free lunch."

Milner yelled, "Keep your mouth closed!"

Scott yelled back, "You're not the one about to be eaten by a crazy rat!"

The deputy laughed and shouted out to Milner, "Don't worry, if your friend doesn't talk, then you're next, and maybe she'll place him on, shall we say a more delicate place than your stomach? With all the fallout and shit, we may be doing you a favor, you wouldn't want to have three-eyed kids would you?"

Milner shook as he shouted, "Scott, remember our orders."

"You ain't the one about to be lunch for the rat."

Maynard asked his radio officer, "How long has it been since we lost the signal from Milner and Scott?"

"Sir, it's been a little over an hour."

"Hmm, long enough for the two of them to get into trouble. Let's saddle up and find them before they screw the pooch so badly, we can't repair it."

"Yes, sir. I'll alert everyone."

"Ten minutes, and we roll. We're going through their roadblock and through the tunnel. I want our two men back."

Scott screamed and tried to twist his body off of the table, but he was tied so tightly all he accomplished was cutting his body where the ropes tied him down. He screamed, "Please don't do this! I'm ready to talk..."

The deputy shook his head. "I don't believe you." He nodded to the woman with the cage. "Slowly pull the bottom pan out and give your pet a little taste of the grease... and our new friend."

Scott cried and screamed when the rat bit him a couple of times. "Push the pan back in. Let's see if he's ready to tell us the truth."

Scott shouted, "I'm army!"

The deputy shook his head. "You'll have to do better than that. Who's army?" He nodded to the woman. "Once again to make sure he understands what happens when he lies."

Scott screamed, "The US Army!"

The deputy slowly walked around the table as blood from the bites ran down Scott's side and off the side onto the floor. "Look at the mess you're making. I ought to make you lick up your own blood. There isn't any more US Army, they died in the war."

"There is. I'm not lying. Most of us were in Ukraine or Europe, but we were ordered home after the war. Most who were in Europe died when the Russians nuked the continent. Those of us that were in the Pacific and Korea survived and were brought home on Navy ships."

The deputy looked at Scott. "Were you in Ukraine when the Russians nuked it?"

"I was on a train as a replacement when the balloon went up. There's not a lot of us left, but we are Army, check my dog tags."

He was interrupted by Maynard yelling on the loudspeaker. "Hey in the tunnel, this is LT Maynard of the US Army. If you have my two soldiers, send them out unharmed and I promise I won't roll through the tunnel with guns blazing, and by that, I mean miniguns and 30 mm cannons. I'll give you five minutes to have them in front of the tunnel."

The deputy looked at Scott. "By the good Lord, it sounds like you were telling the truth. Let me help you. We can still be friends. There's no need for your LT to come in here killing everyone."

Scott had a large bandage covering the bites, and he was given a handful of antibiotics to stop any infection. "That rat was clean; you shouldn't get sick. He only nipped you," said the deputy.

"Nipped me? BS, he was eating me."

"No, he wasn't. I can show you some bodies that he did feed on if you want."

Maynard was happy to see his two soldiers coming out, then his eyes homed in on the bandage on Scott. "What happened?" he asked.

"Sir, I got into a little disagreement with a rat."

"A rat?"

"Yeah, a rat. Ain't nothing wrong. I'm good to roll."

The Sheriff walked toward the LT and said, "Sir, I think we should have a little chat."

Chapter 7

Two captains had the unenviable task of providing me with my morning intelligence update. I felt sorry for them because I often took my frustrations out on the messengers, rather than acting like a general officer who keeps his temper in check. The captains rotated the task of sitting in front of me and giving me my morning brief. None of the news was good. My heart was broken as it felt as if we were sliding into the abyss. Our people were sick and hungry. Most didn't have access to clean water. There weren't even common over-the-counter medicines like aspirin.

Winter would soon be on us, and the 'experts' said this year's winter was going to be very bad due to the nuclear winter effect. I didn't know if I believed them or not, only time would tell if the theory would be proven true. I did know that many of our people didn't have sufficient shelter to survive a normal winter, let alone a bad one.

I had an idea; one I almost certainly knew the President was going to reject. We didn't have the resources to protect those in the north from the ravages of winter, so why not bring most of them south where the winters were milder, and they could assist the farmers and help with rebuilding? I also suggested we have a census as soon as possible so we'd know how many people we had and how to create a new House of Representatives. The House numbers were based on population, the Senate was comprised of two Senators from each state. One issue post the war was some states barely had enough people to be considered a town. Should they get two Senators? What about the new states from Canada?

I knew in the pit of my stomach that if we sent census counters out now, they would be attacked by survivors who wanted to know where FEMA and the DHS were with their help. Anyone who showed up in the overcrowded refugee camps would be torn apart. "We're here from the government." That would be the last sentence many would speak. The one report that scared the daylights out of me was hearing that some areas of the country had even resorted to cannibalism. We needed the inventory of MREs stored in Indiana yesterday. Not only did we need an inventory, but we also needed to get them into the hungry hands of our people.

The loss of Captain Gold's people put a huge dent in the plan to distribute them to the survivors. I couldn't change Major Rand's orders without pissing the President off. The loss of over two hundred people was a real problem. We didn't have the numbers to replace Gold's company. We would soon, as every day saw our numbers grow as members of the military got the message to find their way here.

We'd dropped leaflets off to the farmers telling them to scrape the top three to six inches of topsoil off before they planted, but I heard this suggestion didn't go over very well. Some local farmers had responded by dumping a couple of tons of potentially radioactive topsoil in front of the base's main gate. The attached note told us where we could shove our topsoil.

I didn't blame them, and I had ordered no action be taken against the farmers. Instead of being angry with them, I sent troops to help them. I had no experience in farming, and I didn't realize the top few inches were where all the nutrients were. Without the nutrient-rich topsoil, many crops couldn't grow. We needed every ounce of food crops to feed the hungry survivors. We also needed to feed the food animals if we expected to have herds of them in the future. We needed to get the animals to reproduce so we had enough meat for our people.

I prayed the President would select an experienced farmer to be the Secretary of Agriculture. I was a warrior. The only thing I knew about farming was how to dig up the fields to create defensive fighting trenches and how to kill feed animals to feed my troops. I was the wrong person to have to be the acting Secretary while I was also the Secretary of Defense.

The two captains knew I hadn't been listening to them. I was processing information in my head. They stopped the brief until I looked at them and nodded that I was ready to continue.

They picked right up as if I hadn't been sitting across from them for thirty minutes not paying any attention. Russia was a dead country, and the Chinese had hopefully learned their lesson not to screw with us. Most of us thought we were safe and could rebuild. Of course, the question of where and what to rebuild was a daily debate. Most of our cities had been destroyed.

Some were still 'hot,' as in the radiation levels were high enough to cause fatal radiation poisoning.

The captains repeated the demands the surviving governors had made for instructions and support. The only surviving governor of a major state who was silent was the governor of Texas and that scared me. I knew what he was planning. The last thing we needed right now was to fight another civil war. It could be the last straw that would split the country into small nations. We didn't have the troops to fight a civil war and help the rebuilding at the same time. I was worried that the Warlords would decide they liked being on top of the pyramid and would declare their territory as a new nation. We had to capture Letts and make an example of her so others would know they either played ball or they'd suffer like they never had before. Once we had Letts in custody, we could make a deal with the others.

I thought the President had an excellent idea when he decided to place the new capital in the middle of the country, and thus the need to secure the route to the mines under Kansas City. The scouting was taking much longer than our worst-case projections.

Today's morning report was very sobering. I expected we'd find gangs, but I didn't expect to find Warlords who ruled over vast amounts of our country. I thought we had acted quickly enough to stop violent people from taking over. Huge areas of our country were now part of something similar to a feudal system. I'd read that there was even a person in the ruins of New York City who called himself a king and had appointed dukes and knights. While that king wouldn't live long, he would be copied across the country until we put their courts down. This could be worse than a civil war. This was getting out of control. We needed to show we were still a functioning federal government and that we were supporting the rebuilding efforts. We needed to use our military to keep the roads usable and bring order to where there is lawlessness.

I peppered the captains with questions and requests for data on how many jump-qualified people we had. I knew we had the planes. We had more planes than we had crews to fly. My plan was to drop a couple of hundred troops onto the mine in Indiana to secure the MREs and the freeway leading up to the place. Once both were secure, the C-130s could land and pick up the tons of MREs. The crews would then attach parachutes to the pallets and drop them into the refugee tent cities. It would be like manna from heaven. We might be able to save hundreds of thousands of lives.

Depending on the number of jump-qualified people we had, I wanted to send a squad to each of the tent cities to provide some security and see what else they needed. I also ordered cases of M4 assault rifles, magazines, and ammo be dropped with the squads. My hope was that they would find experienced vets in the tent cities or members of the Guard. There might even be members of local police and sheriffs in the camps. I knew I was taking a huge risk, as the tent cities might be controlled by Warlords who could overwhelm our troops as they landed. I'd then be guilty of arming our enemies. It was a massive risk, but one I thought was worth it. If we could recruit a few people in each camp, we might be able to stop the Warlords from spreading out.

My intelligence reports told me that most of the Warlords came into power by controlling the supply of food and clean water. They had the weapons to control the locals who were quickly disarmed by their troops. If my plan worked, we would be re-arming the people and providing them with the food and leadership needed to overthrow the Warlords. It was a risk, but so is life. I decided not to tell the President until we knew the results. I had a feeling he'd reject the plan due to the risk of the rifles falling into the wrong hands.

Therefore, I selected what I thought was a safe camp to test the program on. If I could show the President a successful mission, I know he'd approve of it being ramped up. I simply had to pick the right tent city for the test. Just as the two captains were leaving, thinking they had escaped without any backblast, I told them to wait a minute. I saw beads of perspiration appear on their foreheads, as they began to worry that I was about to give them some impossible mission or rip them to shreds for something in their report.

"Why don't the two of you sit and listen to an idea I had? I need your help in ensuring our initial run is successful, so the President approves it."

I saw the younger captain's right eye twitch. She was clearly nervous. There were stories of captains who found themselves on the front line after telling me something I didn't want to hear. I wasn't that bad though in reality. I usually transferred those I didn't have my full confidence in to a different post. I was the one who started the rumors about being transferred to the front lines fighting the Warlords though. It helped to keep them in line.

I asked them to review all of the tent cities we'd cataloged and determine which ones were as yet untouched by a Warlord. The younger asked, "Sir, what if our intelligence is faulty and we end up giving M4s to the very people who want to kill us?"

I leered at her. "Since the intelligence comes from your shop, if it's proven to be faulty then the two of you will lead the strike to put the local Warlord down and retrieve our weapons. See how easy that's going to be? I want to get this plan completed quickly so you're both dismissed, and I'll see you in two hours with your recommendations. You're both captains, so be brave and smart, and select the best tent city to demonstrate that the plan will succeed. Don't be like a typical S2 and be wishy, stand in front of me and support your decision. That's all for now."

I knew I'd put the fear of God in them. They needed to toughen up in this new world of ours. I'm trying to force the staff officers to become line officers. We need officers who will lead troops into battle and protect our people. We need them more than we need staff. I want the staff to get their uniforms dirty. I want them to see and experience the cold hard truth of the situation we're in. Maybe then, they'll come up with some new plans and ideas on how we can save the Union. Listen to me, "Save the Union,"

I sounded like I was a Union Officer in 1860.

I have one innovation to help me figure out which officer's plan was good, or if they were just lucky. Don't get me wrong, luck has won more battles than good plans. We discovered a warehouse loaded with the Fitbit Charge 8. These would record the stress levels of the officers selected to lead the teams in the field. I could finally see who was calm under fire and who soiled themselves at the first sound of fire coming in their direction. I love data.

"Naperville? Are the two of you crazy? Naperville is a suburb of Chicago. There were more loose guns floating around Chicago before the war than I could count. Are you sure the surviving gangs from Chicago didn't settle in the refugee camp? This sounds like a poor selection. Explain to me why you selected Naperville."

The young captain, Lilly Cross was visibly sweating. "Captain Cross, you have the floor."

She looked at her partner who nodded toward her. "Sir, we selected Naperville because we reviewed the recordings and noticed there is a core of armed people who fought back two gangs from entering the camp six days after the war. We believe that if your plan is to convince the President, it should be in a location he and others assume would be impossible to succeed in like a suburb of Chicago."

"Are you willing to bet your lives on Naperville?"

Both captains looked at each other and nodded. Cross looked at me and replied, "Yes, sir. We are."

"Good. Then the two of you will lead the first mission to its success. You will be supported by two SpecOps squads of twelve people in each. In addition, there will be fifteen members of the 101st in case you get into trouble. Meet me in the conference room in thirty minutes.

The captains looked like they'd seen a ghost. I refused to answer any of their questions. "Conference room in thirty."

Once settled, I started the brief, "You will leave tomorrow at 0230. That will put you over Naperville at dawn."

Captain Cross looked scared. "Sir, we've never jumped before."

"There's no time to train you so don't worry about it. Your chute, like everyone else's, will be connected to the plane, so when you jump it will automatically pull your chutes open."

"What happens if something happens, and the chute doesn't open?"

"Do you believe in God?"

"Of course, I do. My father was a preacher."

"Then I suggest you pray on your way down. If your chute doesn't open, maybe he'll drop you in a hay pile. If not, then at least you get a chance to ask him why he didn't drop you in one. Time is running out. There isn't time. to teach you when and how to use a reserve chute so you'll reply on the main. To be honest with you, the odds of the main not opening are so small it's not worth talking about. Here are overheads of the camp and maps of the area. I suggest you visit the range and make sure you remember how to use an M4 and the M17 side arm."

At 0230 the two captains were led into the first C17. They noticed two other C17s that were waiting for their plane to taxi to the runway. Captain Cross began asking Captain Lewis who led the Special Forces teams, "Sir..."

"You don't have to call me sir; we're the same rank. What's on your mind?"

"What does it feel like when we jump?"

"You'll believe a man, or in your case a woman, can fly."

Cross ran to the restroom and tossed everything that had been in her stomach. Three hours later, she stood in the open doorway of the plane when the green light flashed on. She knew she couldn't jump, but that's when she felt two strong arms push her into the sky as the sun began rising over the horizon. She screamed as her chute opened. No one had warned her that she would be pulled up when the chute opened. She threw up again and landed in a tree.

Captain Lewis looked up at her hanging from a large branch. "At least she didn't break a leg or an ankle." His sergeant smiled. "Want me to climb up and cut her loose?"

"Yeah, my orders were to keep an eye on her. Typical REMF, but orders are orders."

Over two hundred people at the tent city stared at the rows of parachutes landing in the field fifty yards from the small city. Some thought they were being invaded until they saw one of the soldiers floating down waving a large American flag. Some of them started cheering that help had arrived. They saw palettes hanging under large parachutes. People ran from tent-to-tent waking others. "Help is here! Help is here. They're falling from the sky!"

Captain Lewis ordered a large white tent with a red cross on it to be set up while ten others unpacked the mobile kitchen. Lewis picked up the megaphone. "Good morning, Naperville. I am US Army Captain Lewis, and we are here with a team of doctors and nurses, a field kitchen to dish out hot food, and of course, coffee and weapons so no one can cause you harm. Please allow the injured to reach the medical tent before meals are served. For those reporting to the med tent don't worry about missing a meal, once we have a count, we will have your breakfast brought to you."

Lewis didn't need a loudspeaker to hear the cheering from the thousands in the tent city.

Chapter 8

Captain Gold had to be restrained in the back seat of Crockett's truck because she constantly attempted to escape. She answered every question put to her with the same four words: "My name is Captain." She either refused or was incapable of answering any questions. Crockett left half of his squad to slowly continue their hunt for the Warlord Letts while he and the other half of the squad drove Captain Gold to the nearest FOB which was also a field hospital.

"Paging Master Sergeant Crockett, paging Master Crockett, please report to the lobby."

"Master Sergeant?"

"Yes, that's me."

"Hello, I'm Doctor Parsons, I'm Captain Gold's doctor. Why don't we meet in my office? It's just down the hall."

"Fine, I'll follow you."

"Would you like a coffee?"

"Yes, thank you."

"I can't make it through my shift without coffee. Many who come here pay in coffee or corn. Some even bring us a pig to pay their bills. Times have changed. There's no insurance companies anymore. We're in a new world, one I'd hoped never to see, let alone live in, but here we are. Sergeant, I understand you brought her here. Can you tell me where you found her?"

"I didn't find her, she found us. Or the people who had her let her loose close to us, so we'd find her. Can you tell me her condition?"

"She has suffered a stroke that appears to have been brought on by the improper use of a mixture of drugs. We don't know the combination used; we can only estimate, but that's all. The drugs pushed her blood pressure so high; she had a bleed in her brain. It's the same as if she'd had a serious stroke. We had to open her skull to release the pressure from her swollen brain. It should return to normal in a few days."

"Can you repair the damage?"

"I have stopped the bleeding but there's no telling what the future holds for her. If she is strong, she may reclaim some of who she was when the brain begins to create new pathways around the damaged part of her mind."

Crockett shook his head. "Doctor, I thought the brain couldn't heal itself."

Doctor Parsons replied, "On one hand you're correct. The brain doesn't heal like a cut, so the damage that is caused by a bleed or clot is permanent. But if the patient is strong enough, the brain can create new pathways for information to flow around the damaged areas. Before I came here to help treat victims of the war, I was a neurosurgeon in Tulsa. I was on vacation with a couple of friends fishing when the war started. A week later I had a new job: ER doctor treating the worst wounds you can imagine." The doctor looked into Crockett's eyes. "I take that back because looking at you, I believe you most likely have seen worse than I treated." The doctor swallowed half a cup of hot black coffee in two mouthfuls then looked at the ceiling. "The burns are the worst. I've never seen anything like them. People's skin just melted. The skin on the fingers melted together, eyes, noses, and ears missing. It was as if the sun exploded over the city. We couldn't do anything for them. Before the war there were maybe two or three hundred burn centers in the country; afterward, there are zero. We ran out of sterile bandages in the first day, more like after the first couple of hours." The doctor poured himself another cup of coffee.

Crockett let the doctor talk; he knew he needed a shoulder to tell his story. He waited until the doctor was finished with his second cup. "Doctor, are there any numbers? I mean what are the odds of her brain being able to rewire itself?"

"That's an excellent way to think of it. Yes, rewiring. Much depends on the patient themselves. Much of it depends on the strength of their willpower. The power of the mind is unbelievable."

"Is there anything I or anyone else can do to help her rewire her brain?"

"Who does she care about? Parents, siblings, spouse, lover? The closer the person is to her, the better chance they will have of breaking through and helping her. There is one other issue you need to be aware of."

Crockett never feared battle, and yet right now he felt a cold shiver race down his spine. "Sir?"

Doctor Parsons continued, "She screams every time we attempt to insert an IV. We've attempted to use restraints because she shakes and tosses around in her bed. Once, she even managed to get loose, and security had to subdue her. She keeps repeating 'my name is Captain.' I don't believe she had a natural stroke at all. I believe she has been treated with a series of drugs."

"So, such drugs exist?"

"They're usually used as a truth serum, but they typically leave people without a memory and in a state of high anxiety."

"Do the drugs they used on her stay in the body for any length of time? Will they wear off and return her too normal?"

"Typically, yes, unless they were used in a very dangerous dose, which is what I believe we're dealing with here. There was serious damage to her mind. I can show you the scans..."

"That's okay, I wouldn't understand what they mean."

"Take my word for it, they are not pretty. Someone intentionally destroyed her mind."

"I see. Sir, could I have a copy of your report?"

"I'd like to, knowing you'd take revenge on whoever did this to her, but the law forbids me from sharing her medical records with anyone without her express permission, and we both know she's in no condition to even know where she is, let alone to give her consent. I have other patients I need to attend to now. Please help yourself out."

Crockett watched the doctor lay Captain Gold's report on his desk. He nodded to Crockett. "If you'll excuse me, I have to make the rounds."

Crockett understood what wasn't said. He picked up the report, folded it, and slipped it into his armored vest. He walked out of the medical tent cursing Letts, whispering to himself, "Bitch, no matter where you're hiding, I'm going to find you and I'm going to make you suffer. Maybe I'll use your own drugs on you, and you'll be committed to a nut house for the rest of your days without knowing where you are. That may be the least I do to you. You're not going to slip through my fingers this time. You're going to pay for your crimes. You're going to suffer like you were already in Hell."

Crockett walked out of the tent and climbed into his truck.

His driver asked, "Where to boss?"

"The command vehicle. I have a call I don't want to make, but one that needs to be made. I'm going to need a really stiff drink when that call ends."

"I'll make sure we have your favorite."

Rand listened to Crockett's report. His face was drained of color as he absorbed Gold's medical information. "Master Sergeant, I have one question for you."

"Sir?"

"Can you find her?"

"Yes, sir."

"Then you know what to do. Keep me informed and please ask the doctor to give me a call at the end of every day with a progress report."

"Sir, he explained that there won't be much progress for a while. He did suggest that, if possible, you should visit her. She might recognize you and it could help her to rewire her brain."

"I have a better idea. Are you still at the medical tent?"

"Yes, sir."

"Good. I'm sending orders to have him, and Captain Gold transferred here. We have a better stocked MASH unit than his. Maybe we have something that counteracts whatever they gave her."

"I'll inform him before continuing my search for Letts."

"Master sergeant, if possible, I want her alive."

"Sir, so do I. So do I."

Maynard covered his nose with his wet handkerchief. The smells from the tunnel choked him up. He tried not to show his suffering as he reached into his pack and withdrew a small container of Vicks VapoRub and rubbed it under his nose. The strong scent of the rub blocked most, but not all of the smells from the tunnel. It was a combination of body odor, vomit, urine, and feces, but there was another stink, one he was far too familiar with, that of death. There were lanterns in the front ten percent of the tunnel. These were the lights that had led him to mistakenly believe that the tunnel had power. He used his flashlight to look deeper into the tunnel. The beam of light told him a story he'd wished he hadn't seen.

The tunnel was full of people, most looking like skeletons, their skin pulled tightly over their bones. Many hadn't seen a full meal since the war. There was a section of the tunnel filled with people lying on the cold road surface; some were rolling around moaning. Maynard knew they were suffering from radiation poisoning, and he knew that over the next few days, none would survive. Many were lying in their own waste.

Radiation poisoning was a horrible way to die. The body's organs shut down, and blood seeped and flowed from the mouth, ears, eyes, and anus. The conditions got worse for three or four days, and then there were two good days. These were followed by the body giving up as the bone marrow and the organs died. The victims lost their hair, and even their teeth. They couldn't keep anything in their stomachs; anything they attempted to eat came back up, further weakening them. Finally, when they couldn't take the suffering any longer, they died. Given the war had ended months ago, these people were exposed to a high dose of radiation recently. He wanted to find out where it was, so he didn't send the President through it.

Maynard walked the entire 1.5 miles, the full length of the tunnel. He asked his guide, "How many?"

"I'm not going to lie to you, I don't know. The numbers change every day. Some die, others find their way here and, some just disappear."

"Disappear?"

"Yes, sir. We don't take any form of attendance; we try to provide a safe place for the survivors."

Maynard looked at his guide. "A safe location to die?"

"Is there any safe place to die? We have almost no food or clean water. We do the best we can."

"I have some MREs and bottled water you can have. I wouldn't let any of those suffering from radiation poisoning have a MRE, they will only waste them when they throw them back up. If you have any soup, give that to them. They might be able to hold the soup down; the MREs are too rich and heavy for them."

"Yes, sir. We do have some soup. Are there any other orders?"

"What do you do with the bodies?"

"We toss them into the woods on the sides of the tunnel."

"I can smell their rot. They need to be buried or dumped deeper into the woods."

"Yes, sir. I'll take care of it. Is there anything else?"

"Yes, I need a lane opened through the tunnel so my vehicles can transit the tunnel. We need to reach the loop around the city."

"That's going to take some time."

"Time isn't something I have. I'm under the Secretary's direct orders. I can't break my orders so I need you to open a lane so my vehicles can transit the tunnel."

"Yes, sir. I'll get right on it."

Chapter 9

Rand told his aide to get him to their old FOB as quickly as possible so he could meet the helicopter that was bringing Captain Gold and Doctor Parsons to the upgraded medical facility. Helicopters were rare after the war. It took a call to me for Major Rand to get permission to use one to bring the captain and doctor back. They were so rare because most had been destroyed on the ground or knocked out of the sky when the Russian nukes exploded.

Rand's aide got a pickup with additional armor and three heavily armed escorts in the pickup's back seat. A new minigun chambered in 6.8mm was mounted in the truck's bed. The roads had been cleared so they were able to make the return trip in one hour and not the four it had taken them to get to their first checkpoint.

Rand, surrounded by his security team, watched the Blackhawk begin its landing process. A large white circle had been spray painted on the grass fifty yards from the MASH unit. Rand moved back so he wasn't torn apart by the helicopter's blades.

The Blackhawk had a large red cross painted on its doors.

The first person who jumped out of the bird was Doctor Parsons. He motioned to the four orderlies to approach the helicopter. "She's sedated, it was the only way we could get her on the gurney. Be careful with her. She tends to get very violent when she sees anyone approaching her with a syringe. She doesn't look it, but she is very strong and can lash out quicker than you expect. She knocked out three orderlies at my facility."

Rand quietly approached the gurney. "Hey baby, it's me. Everything is going to be okay. Rest now. No one here will hurt you."

He was surprised when her eyes opened, she began to struggle, and then she focused on his face. She relaxed and tried to reach over to touch Rand. He reached down and patted Gold's face. Doctor Parson smiled. "That's the first good sign I've seen from her. Someplace in her tortured mind she remembers you. Can I assume you were... are... more than friends?"

"We knew each other from jump school. We are more than friends. We love each other."

"Good. That's very good. That means there's hope for her. I have a lot of work to do. Can I get you to return and help me bring her back?"

"I'm leading a special mission for the President. I will find a way when you call. I can't promise I'll be able to spend a lot of time here. How about I make a few videos for her, things only she and I would know."

"That could be very helpful. When can you make them?"

"I'll start tonight. I'll send them to you over the encrypted link. Please don't share them with anyone."

"Of course. I am only sharing her condition with you because you're the only one who is close to her. I understand she lost all of her family in the war?"

"That's correct. They lived in LA, which is now a smoking hole in the ground... actually, as I understand it, it's more like five smoking holes. No one in LA County survived. If the bombs didn't kill them, the fallout did, or the lack of clean water, lack of food, and the gangs fighting to control the debris. She and I only had each other to hold onto after the war."

Doctor Parsons asked, "What happened to your family? Did they die in the war too?"

"Mine died when a drunk driver ran a red light and plowed into their car as they were on their way to celebrate my promotion to captain."

"I'm very sorry. Major, when you make the videos, please make sure to show either your face or an item that's very important to her, something she would instantly recognize. Can you do that?"

"I have a few special items. I'll hold them next to my face. Will that help?"

"I hope so. The damage to her brain was very severe. I'm hoping her subconscious pushes her to come around. Major, if she does, it's going to be very important that you show up next to her. We'll help you to bring her around."

"Doc, we're still fighting, and as I said, I'm on a mission for the President. I can't drop everything and run back here if we're in the middle of a firefight."

Doctor Parsons stepped close to Rand. "Major, if you ever want to see her as the woman you knew, and I assume still love, then you'll find a way to be here when I call. If I have to, I'll call your boss to get you detached from your mission. Our best chance of finding Letts who did this to her is what's locked up inside of her."

"I understand. I'll contact the SecDoD and see if he agrees."

"Major, remember what I said. You're her last and only chance of returning to you as you knew her. She's trapped in her nightmares. I can try to bring her back, but she didn't respond calmly to anyone or anything until she saw and heard you. You hold the key to unlocking what happened to her. I assume you still care for her?"

"Of course, I do. I wouldn't be here if I didn't."

"I know she's under your command now and things could get sticky. Should I contact your boss and explain the situation?"

"Why don't we place the call together. That way, if he has any questions, we can address them together."

I listened to the major and doctor. "Major, do you believe you can continue your mission and still provide the doctor with what he needs to bring Captain Gold back to the land of the living? I know of your relationship. I assume that if she can be brought back, then you'll be able to act professionally."

Rand leaned in so the mic could pick his words up and I'd clearly hear him. "Sir, of course I can. I only want what's best for all of us."

"Good. Doctor, let me know if there's anything I can do for you. I want to know what's locked in her head. If we have any opportunity to capture Letts, she holds the key and I want that door unlocked. That Warlord has and is costing us too many problems. If we're going to save this country and have any chance of restoring who we were, then we have to bury every one of these so-called Warlords. Major Rand is commanding a mission that is very important to the President. He has to complete that mission. I can buy him some time by saying he's got a hot lead on taking Letts down, but that will only work for a short time. Doctor, you need to find a way to unlock Captain Gold's memory, then I can end Letts' reign of terror and murder. I learned she's also restarting slavery and she's expanding her area. If we don't stop her, we'll be fighting a new civil war that will burn the country down. We'll never be able to survive."

Doctor Parsons nodded his head. "Mr. Secretary, I understand. I'll do my best."

I smiled. "Doctor, remember, time isn't our friend."

"Sir, it's not hers either."

Rand shook Doctor Parson's hand. "Do you mind if I borrow your bird to return to my people?"

"Not at all. I don't know if the pilot will mind, but since it's not my bird, borrow it all you want. I suggest you return it in one piece. I had to bend a lot of arms to get the use of the bird, and then I had to get someone to put the red crosses in red tape on the doors."

"Good. So, they're only tape. It'll be easy to remove them when I keep it."

"Good luck with that. Your boss who was just on the phone will be asking me for it back."

"Whoa, you didn't tell me that's who you borrowed it from."

"Major, who else would have access to a Blackhawk? This is the first one I've seen since the day of the war."

"I hope he doesn't mind that I'm taking it. If I have to come back and forth, this is the only way I'll be able to. Every hour we'll be getting further and further away."

"Can I ask where this further and further place is?"

"Do you have a current TS/SCI?"

"No, do I need one?"

"I'm sorry, but you do, or I can't answer."

"Major, in that case, enjoy his bird and good luck. I hope to see you soon."

"Doctor, here is my personal email, please let me know of her progress."

"I will. Thank you for coming."

Rand jumped on the Blackhawk and gave the pilot the coordinates to his people. While in the air, the pilot said, "Major, you've got a radio call. Want to switch with the co-pilot?"

"This is Major Rand, go ahead on encrypted channel 18."

"Major, this is Captain Miller, sir, we have a small situation, and we could use your expertise. Can I send your pilot our coordinates?"

"Can I ask what the problem is?"

"Sir, it's very hard to explain. It would be easier if you saw it for yourself."

"Send the coordinates to the pilot." Two minutes later, the pilot replied, "Major, I've got them. Should we head to these new coordinates?"

"Might as well see what spooked the captain. What will be our ETA?"

"Twenty-four minutes."

Upon landing, Rand was met by Captain Miller, who was clearly spooked by something.

Miller said, "Sir, if you would follow me into the terminal."

Rand looked around. "This is an airport?"

"Sir, it used to be, before the war. It was small, usually only two flights in and out every day. Then on Monday, a week ago, they moved in, and their numbers continued to grow by the day."

"Who are they?"

"Let me show you." Rand followed Miller up the stairs and then he stopped speechless. Captain Miller said, "Sir, look around."

Rand stopped and looked around, slowly nodding his head. He saw a mob of people milling around the terminal. "Oh, my Lord. I see what you mean. Where did these people come from?"

"Sir, that's just it, they came from different places. They all ended up living here. They've taken over the terminals and even the hangers to stay out of the elements. No one lands here anymore. Yours is the first plane they've seen since the night of the war. Oh, and one more thing: they told me that there are an additional fifty thousand in transit."

"Fifty thousand?"

"Yup, fifty thousand. We attempted to represent you and the current rules instituted by the President three days ago, but they're in no mood to listen. I want to warn you, they don't like to talk to the 'normals.' Which is what they call us: the people who weren't affected by the nukes."

"It looks like most won't make a day or two. What's their backup plan?"

"You're here now. I'm going to dump the problem in your hands."

"How will I tell who I'm supposed to meet with tomorrow?"

"I'll collect you before it's time."

Rand looked at the jam-packed main terminal with more people arriving every day and he turned to Miller. "Is everyone here damaged by the bombs?"

"Yes, sir. It starts with the lower level where people are blind, have lost parts of their bodies or faces, or have fourth degree burns; many of them look like burnt meat that was left on the grill for hours. Over there on the third level: these people are injured but still able to function. Those in the lowest level are just waiting to die. Those on the second level need help; many already have cancer. Then we have the top level where we are. Many of these people have the pattern of the clothes they were wearing burned into their skin. Some have their fingers and toes burned together; the skin melted and welted together. Some can't talk, see, or hear, but they can tend to themselves."

Rand looked around. "What do they eat? Where does their food come from?"

"The people up here forage for whatever they can find. They've stripped the local towns bare. Clean water is a problem."

Rand pulled a mask over his face. "I'd say sanitation is also a problem. This place smells like a sewer mixed with decay."

Miller nodded his head. "Sir, that's what this place is."

"How do they know to come here?"

"That I can't answer. I know some of the people on this level are doctors and nurses who tend to the worse cases. They ran out of bandages, so they use cut up uniforms they discovered in lockers."

"I also assume they ran out of antibiotics?"

"Yes, sir. They have zero medication left. I'd like permission to give them half of my supplies."

"You can give them one third. We still have a long trek ahead of us, and we're most likely to run into additional ambushes. Those medical supplies may save your like one day."

"Yes, sir. I understand."

"Good. Give them what you and their doctors agree on, and let's get going. We're running way behind schedule. The President is angry enough. I think we need to find a way to make up time before we get hit again. People like these did nothing wrong, and now they're suffering for the sins of Russia and our arrogance. Captain, take a good look at these people. They were the people we swore an oath to protect. We didn't do a very good job, did we?"

Captain Miller lowered his head in shame. "No, sir. We didn't."

Chapter 10

Maynard walked out of the tunnel and into the woods, where he threw up until his stomach was empty. He then sat on a large rock and cried. His sergeant saw him sitting on the rock with his head between his legs and he heard his officer crying. The sergeant didn't know if he should approach him or leave him alone and never mention what he'd seen to him.

He decided to silently walk back to the tunnel, as he slowly shook his head. He remembered the trick Maynard had shown him, and he reached for a small jar of Vicks and rubbed it under his nose. The smell from the dying and human waste managed to break through the Vicks though; it was that bad.

He learned that those who were suffering from radiation poisoning were from the western suburbs of Tulsa. They had been exposed to the clouds of fallout as they made their way along the clogged freeways believing that the tunnels would provide them with safety and security.

Maynard waved his radio operator to him so he could update Major Rand. "Major, I have a sitrep."

Rand replied, "Send it."

"Major, the first tunnel is jammed with survivors. I estimate half of them are the walking dead; they're not even able to walk. They're lying in their own waste and fifth."

"Radiation?"

"Yes, sir."

"Can we traverse the tunnel?"

"Sir, I believe we're going to have to move those too weak and sick into the southbound lane. I offered the person who seemed to be in charge our MREs as payment for their help in moving their people, I don't have enough hands to complete the task by the time the main body arrives."

"Today is your lucky day. I've inherited an almost new Blackhawk."

"Sir, inherited? Who do you know who passed you a Blackhawk?"

Rand laughed. "I sort of *borrowed* it from the Secretary."

"Sir, please don't steal from the boss. I've finally broken you in, I'd hate to start over and break another Major, or God forbid they replace you with a gung-ho LTC."

"LT, how long have you been a First LT?"

"Long enough. I've turned down three promotions. Before the war, I would have been discharged. The old rule of three or out. Either get promoted in one of three boards or you're out. I like being a LT, I don't want to command a company. I like being what used to be called a leader. I know my limitations; I'm leading sixty people. Before the war, I would have led 40."

"You're doing a great job. I was going to promote you..."

"Sir, please don't. I like my job. If you promote me, heaven knows what I'll end up doing if you pin the tracks on me. I like being on point and running the scouts."

"You're right, before the war the rule was three or out. I didn't agree with it. We lost a lot of good people who, like you, were happy with, and good at, their assignments. Today, no one is discharged unless they commit a major crime, and the rumor is, if the offense is serious enough, the condemned are sent to assist recovery teams in the dead zones."

"Sir, not me. I'm asking you to please leave me in place in my current position. I'm indispensable."

"LT, that you are. I'll send you six additional people on the first flight, and I'll continue the flights until you have enough people to clear a lane. I agree that they can't or won't move the sick, so we'll have to."

"Major, a little suggestion: tell those you're sending to bring their gas masks and jars of Vicks."

"Is it that bad?"

"Major, it's a mix of death, rotting meat, old and new vomit, and shit all rolled together."

"Oh my God. Okay, I'll issue that order. Does it help?"

"Well enough to allow us to stay in the tunnel a little."

Rand checked his tablet. "Expect the first flight in thirty minutes."

Maynard was surprised the first person who jumped out of the Blackhawk was Major Rand. He thought to himself, *damn, I wish he would have given us time to clean the tunnel up a little before just dropping in. I could have used a little warning. I guess that's what Majors do.*

Maynard jogged to meet the Blackhawk. "Sir, welcome to my little slice of Hell."

"LT, I couldn't let you have all the fun. Is anyone in charge of the tunnel?

Where's that light coming from? Do they have power? Is there a working plant around here? That would be really good news. We could set up these two tunnels as a FOB."

"Sir, I suggest you hold off on that until you see the inside of the tunnel. The light is coming from candles and a few solar generators that provide them with power to charge devices and camp lanterns. One of them was a big camper, and he brought all sorts of supplies."

"Give me the twenty-five-cent tour."

"Sir, due to inflation, the cost of the tour is now one gas mask."

Rand tossed an extra to Maynard. "I should write you up for not having yours."

"Sir, it was a decision between additional ammo and water, or the mask."

"I understand, but this is a perfect reason why you need your mask."

"Yes, sir. I didn't think I'd be driving into a gas attack."

"Now let me see the tunnel. The main body is two hours behind me."

Rand walked out of the tunnel, bent over, and threw up everything that had the misfortune to be in his stomach. His body shook: something it hadn't done since his first battle in the GWOT. He slowly walked to where Maynard stood looking back toward the tunnel. "LT, I suggest we see what can be done for the survivors. I agree with you that most in the rear third aren't going to make it. I'll talk to the doc about how he can make their last couple of days less painful."

"Sir, an overdose?"

"I'll leave the how up to them and the doc. If it was me, I'd rather go in sleep than suffer until my body gave out. I feel so sorry for them. I'd take their suffering away from them if I could. I do have an out-of-the-box idea: I want you to find me a few addicts."

"Sir? Addicts?"

"Yup. We're going to get some drugs. We don't have sufficient inventory to take everyone's pain away without using up all of our opiates; drugs our people might need in combat. The doc can use the drugs to help the worst of the cases in there."

"Yes, sir. Addicts. I'll put a couple of the younger men and women on it. They're sure to know where to score drugs. I'll explain why we need them."

"I don't want to catch anyone using. If I do, they'll suffer my full wrath, and they don't want to see me pissed, am I clear?"

'Yes, sir. I'll make it very clear to them."

"Tell them to check the houses. If any of them had teens living there, they may have drugs hidden inside."

"I'll send four to begin a search."

"Remind them to hurry. Tell them that the doc will be here with the lead elements of the convoy, and the President is burning up my phone with texts asking when we're going to reach KC. I'm going to use the space in front of the tunnel as our camp for tonight."

The doc assigned to the convoy sat across from Rand in his tent. "You want me to OD them?"

"I want you to ask them if they'd like their pain to stop. Both of us know they're fatal, and they have less than a week of very painful days ahead of them. A small amount of Fentanyl will take their suffering away. They'll just drift into the blackness."

Maynard was worried. "Sir, isn't that murder or them committing suicide or something?"

"I look at it as mercy."

Maynard looked back at the tunnel. Even from a hundred yards away, the stench filled his lungs, and he knew in his heart that the major was correct. "Based on where we are today, I agree with you."

"I want to get on the road. I'm going to leave twenty-five people with the doc, and I want a platoon of your scouts to escort them when they get back on the road. The President is driving me crazy about finding a safe route; if he saw this, he'd lose his cookies and may take it out on me."

Rand walked to the mess tent to get a mug of coffee when Sergeant Ketts came to him. "Sir, I have some very bad news."

"Is it so bad it can't wait until I get some coffee?"

"No, sir."

Rand took a large swallow and shook his head, thinking, *we've got to locate a source of better coffee. I was hoping Ketts would go away, but I might as well listen to his news.* "Sergeant Ketts, what's your bad news?"

"Sir, we sent a drone to check our course west, and it's returned with some very bad news."

"Out with it."

"Sir, 44 east through the southern end is covered in fallout."

"Surely after all the time that has passed since the war ended, the fallout would have a half-life down to almost zero or at normal background radiation levels?"

"It is close, however..."

Rand raised his hand. "Is it or isn't it close to normal background levels?"

"Sir, my job as the CBN warfare tech..."

"Safe or not?"

"Sir, it's safe if we don't stop and spend any time until we reach the northeast segment of Interstate 44."

"Thank you, I'll remember not to stop for a picnic break until we leave the state. Would that be satisfactory?"

Sergeant Ketts snapped to attention, saluted, and performed a perfect turn, leaving Rand sighing. *Why did I end up with Ketts? Everything is a life-or-death issue with him. On the other hand, I'm glad he warned us not to loiter. I don't know how the Secret Service is going to take it when they escort the President along this route and discover the background level is above normal. Those people have no sense of humor. A few Rads isn't going to hurt anyone as long as they don't stop to sightsee.*

*****

I studied my daily intelligence brief and shook my head. Colonel Red stood in front of my desk. "I thought we dealt a death blow to the cartels when we killed Valdez and took out the leadership of the Texan rebellion?"

"Sir, the cartels got knocked back on their heels. However, they elected a new leader..."

"Elected? I'm sure they didn't hold an election."

"No, sir. One ensured he was the only one running for the position."

"What's their involvement with Texas?"

"The new governor of Texas cut a deal with the new cartel leader allowing them to cross as long as they kept their drugs out of his state. He even laid out a safe route through Texas into New Mexico."

"Okay, I guess it's time to finally put a stop to the cartels in Mexico and have a prayer meeting with the governor of Texas."

"Sir?"

"Watch and learn. Please send General Jeff to me."

Colonel Red raised his eyebrows. "Yes, sir."

"General Jeff reporting as ordered."

I smiled. Jeff was my pit bull and master at destroying our enemies. He was one of the prime authors of the China plan. "General, have a seat. I need you to figure out a plan to destroy the cartels, and by that, I mean I don't want to have to deal with them again. And I want the governor of Texas to know that he's playing with the big boys now."

"Yes, sir. I can do that. Normal 24 hours?"

"Perfect." I smiled knowing I'd have a workable plan tomorrow.

Chapter 11

An hour later, I received two calls, both ruined what might have been a rare, good day. The first was from General Jeff. "Sir, I just sent you a series of pictures taken from our drones, there appears to be a convoy of migrants making their way to the border."

"I thought the migrants gave up on us after the war. Surely, they know they're traveling through hot zones."

"The new cartel boss told the organizers there wasn't anything to fear; that the radiation had died away."

"Why is he sending them here? He must know most of our people are living in tents and homeless shelters because their homes and infrastructure were destroyed. We don't have any sanctuary cities left. If they enter our country, and that's a large IF as we still have armor sitting on the border with orders to keep it closed. This isn't 2023, if they attempt to cut the fence they will be arrested, put to work in the worst locations, and then deported along with their families. How do we get that message across to them before they reach the border?"

Jefferson asked, "Sir, what if we direct them to another border; one that still claims to care."

"I assume you're talking about California, aren't you?"

"You know me very well. Yes, California. They, along with Oregon and Washington, announced themselves as independent countries, so let's help them along. Before the war, they announced they were sanctuary states and welcomed migrants. Since they never rescinded their statements; I believe we should honor their wishes."

"I'll make the arrangements to guarantee they cross at San Diego. Most of the south side of the city and the harbor were destroyed when the base was nuked. A couple of them were ground hits, resulting in massive and very deadly fallout. We'll be leading many to their deaths. Does that bother you?"

"Issue the warnings. Make sure there are signs highlighting the danger at the border in both languages. If they ignore the warnings, then they bring whatever happens upon themselves. We warned them. We posted it in Spanish. If they ignore the warnings, then I'll sleep peacefully knowing I did my part."

"Yes, sir. Should I inform the acting Prime Minister of the People's Union of the West Coast what's coming his way?"

I laughed into the phone. "Like he warned us he was leaving the union, and we could go screw ourselves? NO! Let him find out like we did about his decision. He didn't give his people the option of voting on the question. He wanted to be President, and when he realized the country wasn't going to be able to hold an election for a few years, he decided he owned the ball, and he was taking it home. We stripped every asset we would take. The Prime Minister is on his own and I'm not doing him any favors."

"Yes, sir."

That call wasn't that bad. The second one, the second one, was what I would classify as a level-10 earthquake. President McCarthy informed me that he couldn't wait any longer. He and the Executive Departments were leaving for Kansas in two days. He informed me that I could stay, or I could travel with them.

He hoped I would decide to make the journey with him as he considered me an asset and would miss his daily walks to my office, then he laughed telling me I could use the exercise walking to his office when we arrived at our new home. I tried to talk him out of leaving until Major Rand reported in telling us he had secured the route.

He told me he'd waited long enough. His advisors told him that by leaving, we'd force Major Rand's hand and light a fire under his ass. I attempted to explain all of the issues that were slowing the Major's progress. I heard his CoS telling him the Major had had more than enough time to make it to Kansas and return let alone radio in the route. He told the President not to accept any of my excuses, thus I had 48 hours to light that fire under Rand and hope he wasn't into any trouble that could bite the President on his travel. Damn, I miss the "No, you're not" Secret Service. Where were they when I needed them?

I called the new Director of the Secret Service, who began laying it into me before I could get a word out. I know which side of his bread was buttered. I then called LTC Putilla, the commander of what was left of SOCOM. "Colonel, the President has decided to leave for Kansas in two days."

Putilla responded before I could tell the rest. "I didn't know Major Rand had reached the city and declared it safe."

"Colonel, that's the problem. He hasn't. He's still in Oklahoma."

"Oh boy. I guess you called because you want us to be the President's scouts and make sure nothing happens to him. Are you pulling up stakes and going with him?"

"I don't see that I have any option except to go with him. Get your teams, and before you ask, all of them should be prepared to escort the President. Take all of the ammo you can carry and swap the machine guns out and replace them with the new miniguns. If you run into trouble, the miniguns can end it quicker. I have to make a call to Major Rand. We'll talk every six hours."

"Sir, good luck with that call. I bet I'll be able to hear his reaction over here on the other end of the base."

"No bet. We'll speak again at 22 hundred hours."

I told my acting XO that I wished Moore was still with me, because he'd have handled a load of this crap off my desk, then I said, "Someone get me Major Rand on the secure set."

Rand knew a ton of crap about to fall on him, The Secretary rarely called this early, "Major Rand here for the Secretary."

"Major, this is the Secretary."

"Yes, sir. What can I do for you? Do you have questions on my recent progress report?"

"No. It was very clear. I'm calling because I have news that I wish I didn't have to give you."

"If you're calling to remove me, all I can say is thank you."

"Ha! Don't you wish that was the reason for the call? My news is even more maddening than me releasing you from command. The President and the rest of the government are leaving for the mines in 48 hours."

"No, he can't. We're stuck in Oklahoma."

"The other bad news is he decided not to fly, he wants to see the country and meet the survivors. After he arrives at the mine, he plans to send the rest of the agencies by plane."

Rand looked up at the sky shaking his head, "Sir, he'll land into an unknown situation. I can order the scouts to drive through the night, but there are too few of them to hold the airport and the mines. I can't push the rest of the company there because we're still trying to clear the tunnel, and part of Interstate 44 is a dead zone. The drones are telling us that the road is blocked for at least twenty miles. It's going to take us at least a full day to untangle the loop around Tulsa. Our drones don't have the range to tell us what else we're going to run into when we enter Missouri."

"Major, the President issued a direct order, that wants to be in the mines within a week and then he's going to announce the new capital."

"Sir, we haven't captured Letts yet. When she finds out, and she will, that the President is on the road, she will launch an attack to kidnap him. She's a real tough nail to deal with. I'm sure Master Sergeant Crockett told you the same thing."

I smiled, "I haven't told Crockett yet about the President's plans."

Rand asked, "Isn't there some way you can delay him?"

"Believe me I've run out of excuses. His staff doesn't believe things are as bad I keep telling them."

Rand shook his head, "He's going to find out soon enough. What do you need from me?"

"I need you to complete the mission he and I originally gave you. You have already tasked some people to clear the tunnel and assist the doc in dealing with those who aren't going to make it, so pack up your camp and move. Time isn't your friend. Leave a small number of people every twenty miles. I'm sending you thirty more people; the pilot will contact you when he's thirty minutes from your location."

"Sir, that won't work. My staff informed me that the airport is a mess. We can't clear it in a day or two, not even in a month. If they land there, I can't promise we can provide security for them. There are over 50,000 people jammed in the terminal. Most need medical treatment that we don't have."

Rand disconnected the call and yelled for his staff. "I want us packed and on the road within one hour. One hour, am I clear?"

The staff were shocked as they looked around and began talking over each other. Rand let it go on for one minute before he yelled, "Shut up. You're wasting your time. You're down to fifty-two minutes and counting. No questions. Pack it up."

Captain Brown, who was a recent addition, said, "Sir, it's not possible. It simply can't be done."

"Excellent answer, Captain, you're removed from your position. I believe you used to be my S3. I'm also busting you down to private. Now get out of my tent and cut those bars off your blouse. Does anyone else want to bring up an objection?"

The four other captains looked at each other. Captain Scott said, "Sir, all due respect, we'd like to be excused so we can get this donkey show on the road per your orders."

"Excellent. Go, get out of here."

Rand returned to his small desk that they had taken from an empty school. He didn't pay any attention to his tent being taken down around him as he continued to plot their route. A corporal silently entered and packed Rand's belongings then he asked, "Sir, which personal weapons will you be taking with you?"

"I'll take my M17, four full mags, my backup M18 with two mags, and my M7 with six of the new 30-round mags they dropped to us three days ago."

"Sir, what about the AK next to your rack?"

"Pack it."

One hour and fifty-two minutes later, the convoy left their temporary base. The only sign they'd been there were the tire marks from the trucks. The soldiers had polished up the area to make sure no papers were left behind. Rand was in the first truck, and the last truck of four people drove through the camp to make sure nothing was left behind before racing to catch up with the main body. They took up position two miles ahead of the main body in case someone attempted to sneak up on the convoy. However, they didn't know they were being watched, as the convoy's position was texted back to the headquarters of the Warlord Letts who subsequently plotted their position every five miles. "I think I know where they're going, and we're going to set up a little surprise party for them," said Letts as her staff smiled wickedly. "We're going to set up at this rest stop which is around a blind curve. They won't see us until it's too late."

Chapter 12

Crockett checked the map for the third time. "My gut says Letts used that school building three miles ahead on the left. I want the first squad to check it out but be alert for booby-traps. Don't make the wrong assumption that she's just a wannabe. She's very smart and likes to set traps and ambushes for everyone who attempts to capture her. She's taken down two precious platoons that found her trail; they walked into one of her ambushes, and none survived.

"Keep your eyes open. Starting from a mile before the school, make the assumption that you're already in a minefield, because I've got a hundred that says you won't know you're in one until one of you fools steps on one and blows his legs off. She likes to wound simply because she knows a wounded soldier takes up more resources than a dead one. Staff Sergeant, move out and stay in touch."

After the first squad had moved off toward the school, Crockett addressed the leader of his second squad. "I want you to take your squad and check out the police office a block past the school. Be careful. Assume she's set IEDs throughout the entire town."

The first squad scoped out the school as a PFC pointed to a window. "I saw a wire hanging from the top of the window up there. I'm betting it's tied to a series of IEDs. She must have assumed we'd use the window she left open, and once we did, boom."

Crockett used his binoculars to check the school out. "Yup. Good eyes. Let's toss a large rock through the window and see what happens."

The answer to the rock was instant. As soon as it sailed through the open window, the IED in the room and the one on the roof that was angled down both exploded.

The one on the roof spread hundreds of steel BBs in a semi-circle in front of the window while the IED inside the classroom exploded and blew out the inside walls.

The window frame went sailing twenty-five yards toward the squad members who were watching the fireworks from a safe position.

Crockett smiled. "Toss the largest rock possible though the front door."

The front doors flew out from the IED placed inside the doors.

Crockett said, "I wonder how many IEDs she planted in that damn school. I want to get into it so we can see if she left anything behind, but I don't want to get shredded."

One of the corporals asked, "Why can't we just toss rocks through every window and use their IEDs up."

Crockett nodded. "An excellent idea. Let's get it done and don't miss one single window. Even if the window is cracked hit it with a rock. I hope the IEDs don't destroy anything that she left behind. Do we still have that asshole of a prisoner? If so, then send him inside the school. If there are any trip wires or unmissed IEDs, they'll get him first."

Minutes later, there was an earth-shaking explosion and the roof caved in on the rear third of the school. Crockett shook his head, as he thought, *better him than us.* The dust cloud from the explosion covered the entire squad. "Follow me, and let's see what she left behind to screw with our minds," shouted Crockett as he headed for what was left of the school.

He smiled when he saw the bright red message painted on the wall in front of them. *Ho-ho, you missed me. Better luck next time – like when you open the door to the police station.*

A moment later, the ground shook and the remains of the school's broken windows fell to the floor. Crockett and his team ran outside and saw a dark gray smoke cloud rising above what used to be the police station. He yelled, "B Squad, where are you?!"

"Hey boss, to your right, fifty yards behind the school's large rock that the kids painted messages on."

"Your squad are okay?"

"Of course. Did you think she could trap Delta with those little tricks and IEDs she left behind? I knew the police station was such a juicy target that we would have to search it, so I sent a few drones in to look around. Then boom. One must have hit a trip wire. She did leave us a message. The drone captured it and sent the image to my tablet. Take a look."

"Got you this time. I hope bleeding out is painful. I'm sure our paths will cross again, and when they do, I plan on finishing the job."

Crockett looked at the map, trying to figure out where Letts was and where she would strike next.

*****

Doctor Parsons studied Captain Gold's CT scan, before saying to the surgery nurse, "Let's see if we can manage to zap the clot. Maybe if the pressure is removed from her brain, she will return to us."

The nurse pointed at the CT scan. "Doctor, the clot is in the memory center of her brain.

She may return, but she won't remember who she was or what happened to her unless her brain rewires itself. That clot is large and most likely caused major damage. She's very young to have suffered such a large stroke."

"She didn't suffer a normal stroke; she was chemically treated. I'm not familiar with whatever it was they used on her. If we don't deal with the clot, she'll be a walking vegetable. She won't remember anything and will have to be cared for as long as she lives. Are you ready to start?"

"Okay, in that case, the quicker we move, the better chance we have of her recovering. Do we have any idea how long she has been in her current state?"

The doctor nodded. "I wish we did, but we have no idea. I'm going to assume they cut her loose when they realized they had damaged her, and she was of no further use to them."

Gold lay on the operating table with no understanding of anything except that she couldn't move. She saw the clear plastic mask being placed on her face. Nothing made any sense to her.

She opened her eyes and looked around her surroundings. She was on a bed in a private room. She turned her head and saw a nurse standing next to her. "Hello, can you tell me your name?"

Gold nodded her head, "My name is captain."

"Do you remember anything?"

"My head hurts. I am captain."

The nurse injected a sedative into her IV so Gold could rest and checked the monitors. All of her indicators were in the normal range. She thought that was a very good sign. She was one of a small number of surviving nurses who specialized in stroke cases. She'd cared for hundreds of them, and she knew that each brain reacted differently.

Doctor Parsons stopped by to check on Captain Gold. "Nurse, how is our patient?"

"She opened her eyes, and I could see the confusion in them. I gave her a mild sedative, so she should she sleep for eight hours."

"Good, it will give her brain some time to heal. I don't know what they did to her. I checked her head for abusive head trauma that could have caused the stroke. I didn't find any bruises, so I have no idea what did it. Has her blood work come back yet?"

"Not yet. I'm hoping the lab works around the clock so we get the results before she wakes."

"If the labs come back and they show anything abnormal, call me."

"I will. Good night doctor, I hope you can get some sleep."

"Me too, but call me if there's any change in her condition."

Nine hours later, Captain Gold opened her eyes again. "Where am I? What happened to me? Where's Rand?"

Two nurses ran into her room. "Can you tell us your name?"

"My name is... Karen, yes, I'm sure of it, my name is Karen... Gold. My name is Karen Gold. My rank is Captain. I'm Captain Karen Gold,"

"Karen, can you tell us who you work for?"

"I am a captain in the US Army." She felt around her neck and looked surprised and worried.

"Dog tags? My dog tags are missing."

"Captain, that's okay. We have them."

"I need them, please."

One of the nurses returned and placed the metal chain around Karen's neck. "There you go. Do you feel better?"

"Where am I? What happened to me?"

Doctor Parsons had been standing in the doorway. "Captain, you had a stroke, and I operated on you to remove the clot. You should slowly recover most of your memory."

"I can't remember anything before today."

"Sure, you can. You remembered your name, your rank, that you were in the US Army, and you remembered Major Rand."

"Is he here?"

"Not yet. The doctor went to call him. I'm sure he'll be here as soon as he can be."

"I'm very tired."

"I know. I need you to do one thing before you nap: tell me how many fingers I'm holding up?"

"Three."

"Excellent. What's your name?"

"Karen Gold."

"Excellent. Now, can you move your left foot for me? Now the right."

"Wow, you're doing great. I'm proud of you. Would you like to continue or take a nap?"

"I need a nap."

"Of course. I'll turn the light off, and I won't allow anyone to bother you for a few hours."

She closed her eyes and was deep in sleep before the nurse left the room. Two heavily armed MPs stood guard over the captain. They were wearing body armor, ballistic helmets, and they were armed with M7 assault rifles and M17 sidearms. A special pass was required to enter the captain's room.

Captain Miller called Major Rand. " Sir, she's up! She's talking, and she asked for you."

Rand asked, "Who's up and asking for me?" He'd accepted the fact that Karen, or at least the Karen he knew and loved, wasn't ever returning to him.

"Sir, Captain Gold woke and asked for you."

Rand was shocked into silence. He jumped up and yelled, "Where's my Blackhawk?"

"Bringing people to the tunnel."

"Tell the pilot to pick me up and bring me to the MASH facility."

"Yes, sir."

The Blackhawk landed on the freeway, and Rand and two security guards jumped into it.

"To the MASH base as fast as this little bird can go."

"Sir, without a payload and without missiles hanging in the air, I can manage 185. However, we've had additional fuel tanks installed, so today, we'll be lucky to see 150."

"Then dump some of the weight."

"Sir, how? Most of our weight is fuel and batteries."

"Captain, I don't care. Just start weight dump something."

The pilot turned to his co-op. "If he's not careful, we'll burn out our engines."

Rand replied, "I heard that. Let me be very clear, I don't really care about your engines, I only care about making it there as quickly as possible."

"Major, that's all well and good, but I'm not sure we'll be able to land or take off again."

"Yes, you will. I've texted ahead to get new engines there waiting for us. Now if you don't mind, put the peddle to the metal and move this bird. Run the engines up to the red line and keep pushing them."

The pilot and copilot watched the temperature gauges climb. "If we continue at this speed, we'll burn our engines out. I really hope the Major has pull, because I ain't paying for two new engines."

The co-pilot looked at Rand. "He does, he was hand-picked by the Secretary and the President for the mission he's on. If he said he lined up fresh engines for us, then I believe him, so let's set a new Blackhawk speed record. The engines are on him."

The pilot nodded, "Okay, let's break the governors and set a new speed record."

Rand felt the bird shake as its speed picked up. He smiled and prayed to the Lord for help.

Chapter 13

Rand reached out to hold Gold's hand while she slept. Suddenly, she opened her eyes and said, "Who are you? Why are you touching me?"

Rand pulled his hand back and looked at the doctor, motioning for them to talk in the hall. "I thought you said she was getting better, and she asked for me. What the hell is going on?"

"Major, the brain is a very unusual organ. We don't know all that much about it. Some people have strokes and should recover but they don't, while others shouldn't be able to do anything and they do. Let me tell you about a patient of mine: he's a senior citizen, and he had two small strokes followed by a major one. The bleeding happened in his speech center, and it was so large it also destroyed his prompt memory center. Despite this, within two days, he was speaking well enough to be understood. By all rights, he should never have been able to talk again. He literally willed his brain to rewire itself. He still has some minor issues, but you'd never know he'd had a serious stroke."

"What happened to his memory?"

"He suffers from forgetting what was on the tip of his tongue. He learned some tricks to work around his issue though. I'm telling you this because a lot of the recovery is due to how strong-willed the patient is. I know the captain is a strong-willed woman, because she survived when most would have already given up. Let's give her a couple of days..."

"Doc, in a couple of days I'm supposed to be in Kansas City. I'm under direct orders from the President. I can't hang around here." Rand checked his watch. "My ride is arriving to take me back to my convoy in thirty minutes."

"Are you sure you can't stay?"

"I'm very sure. Would you like to see my orders from the President?"

"No, I believe you. Would you like to check on her one more time before you have to leave?"

Rand sat next to Gold as she napped. His tablet pinged to tell him his helicopter was fifteen minutes out. Suddenly, Gold said, "Rand, is that you? Is it really you?"

Rand jumped out of his chair and rushed to hug Gold. "Yes, it's really me. I've been here for a while. I heard they found you and brought you here."

"Where is here?"

"You're in a surgical MASH unit. The place doesn't matter. What matters is you're here and you're awake."

"You're really here. I had a dream that you were here and were holding my hand. Isn't that funny?"

"It really is..."

"Wait a minute, if you're here, who's leading the convoys to the mines? Did you get replaced? Did the boss demote you? No, that's not it. I see your rank tab, or did you put it on just for me?"

"I didn't get demoted. The boss knows I'm here. Hell, he knows when I take a crap, because he usually wants to talk to me in the mobile SCIF *while* I'm crapping."

Gold smiled. "How long can you stay?"

Rand looked at his watch, while they both heard the Blackhawk flare and land. "That long, huh? Where did you nab a Blackhawk from? Is that a new perk for majors?"

Rand held back tears of joy. "No. I sort of borrowed it from the boss."

Gold smiled. "In other words, you stole it."

"More along the lines of I borrowed it while fully intending to return it when I'm finished with it."

"Sure, you are. Honey, I love you."

"I love you too. Look, I'm really sorry, I have to catch that bird, or I will be demoted, and I don't want to spend the next few years digging shitters."

"Go but promise me you'll return. I'm not good at funerals, so don't go and get yourself killed. I'll never forgive you."

"I promise to come back. I love you too. Since I outrank you, I'm giving you an order."

Gold smiled. "What are my orders?"

"I'm ordering you to rest and get better."

"Yes, sir." Gold's eyes closed and she fell into a deep sleep.

Rand looked at the doctor. "She's improving."

"Major, the next time you see her, she may not remember this. Everything depends on her will to survive."

"She's strong. I have faith that she'll pull this off."

"I hope you're right. Have a safe flight, Major."

*****

Rand smiled like he'd won the billion-dollar lottery as he belted himself into his seat in the Blackhawk. The pilot asked, "Major, good meeting?"

"The best meeting I've attended since the war began. How long is the flight back to the convoy?"

"Sir, they've made a lot of progress since you left."

"Hell, I should have stayed away. Have they crossed into Missouri yet?"

"They did. Captain Miller has done a great job."

Rand nodded. "Have they run into any opposition?"

"Sir, the opposition was very weak, typical roadblocks, two were made from Jersey Walls. The captain was able to talk his way through them. There was a rather unusual event that happened though. The captain wrote a report he wanted you to read before we land."

"Great, did he meet little green men from Mars or something?"

"Sir, the report is on this tablet. He didn't want to transmit it, not even over the encrypted network."

Rand thought there must be something in the report that was very sensitive. He opened the tablet and began reading. "Classification: TOP SECRET, SENSITIVE COMPARTMENTED INFORMATION (TS/SCI). Fifty miles into Kansas we encountered a family comprised of a husband, his wife, and their two sons aged 12 and 15. When we stopped to ask them where they were going, they told us they were from the suburbs of Tulsa. They survived the nuclear strikes on the city because their home was located to the southwest of the city. They sealed their windows and doors with duct tape and survived on canned food and bottled water for one week. Then, they began their long walk. The man, Joe, told us that they wore out their sneakers every few weeks. They managed to get new ones from shops along their route, usually Target or Walmart. They said the food and water were looted, but many of the camping supplies, sneakers, and boots were still on the shelves or in the back. He also told us the pharmacy was torn apart and every pill bottle was missing.

"They were going to what they called SubTropolis. The same location we were ordered to investigate. They claimed they had cousins and friends who lived in Kansas City, and when the alert sounded, they went to the mines. They told me that the mines were full of families, and they were protected by a very heavily armed militia who blocked all access to the place. People who left were not allowed to reenter. The wife, Jennifer, said everyone in the mine worked for the militia and that they worked and got paid in food, water, and the right to live in the mine. She said, it wasn't a perfect solution but it did prove them with food and a roof over their heads.

"If the mines turn out to be full of families, the President can't set up the government there. This militia sounds a lot like the Warlords we've fought before. Jennifer said they wear uniforms and follow someone with a star on the center of his shirt."

Rand thought, *oh crap, this could be a real problem. A general. He must have been the state's National Guard commanding officer, or maybe he was one of us who got trapped in the war and knew of the mines before turning it into his own little fiefdom. If they're heavily armed, they must have had access to a Guard armory, or as the commanding officer of the Guard, he gave them access. I need to check the Guard units based in the surrounding areas. Some might have armor.*

Rand told the pilot to overfly the mine entrance so he could put eyes on it. The pilot responded that he could make one flyby, and only one, based on their fuel situation. Rand approved the pass and prayed that the report wasn't accurate because the President was most likely already on the road. He didn't know where else they could establish their new capital now.

The Blackhawk slowed and began to hover over the main entrance to the mines when the co-pilot yelled, "MANPAD!"

The pilot put the Blackhawk into a turn and began dropping countermeasures to decoy the missile that was guided by the heat of the engines. "Major, hold on, this is going to be close. The damn missile isn't taking the bait."

"Keep dumping them, maybe we'll be lucky."

The co-pilot yelled, "Missile two launched, at our 5 o'clock."

The pilot dumped additional decoys.

Rand saw something almost no one gets to see: the first launched missile striking one of the chaff canisters and exploding. The pilot screamed, "We're catching some of that!"

Rand heard what sounded like rain on a tin roof. "That sound is the debris of the first missile striking the bottom of our bird. So far, we're lucky it didn't hit anything critical.

We're running low on decoys, and we have the second missile on our tail."

They weren't so lucky with the second missile, as it wasn't led off course by the chaff or IR decoys. The pilot saw the missile coming, and just like a fighter pilot, he'd been trained to turn away from it. The advantage he had on a fighter was that he could drop hundreds of feet vertically while the missile had to turn around and re-engage its target.

The pilot lost the missile as he dropped the Blackhawk like a rock. Then the missile ran out of fuel and fell onto the Blackhawk. Rand had already vomited twice from the violent motions of the helicopter when the missile struck in the worst place it could: the hub that held the blades together.

The helicopter fell like a rock, striking trees on its way down. The trees shattered the windshield, killing the pilot and the co-pilot instantly. Rand was also injured in the crash. He had three broken ribs and a broken left wrist. He managed to crawl out of the twisted wreck after checking for a pulse on both of the pilots. Rand prayed his tablet would work so he could call for help. He knew a rescue bird would have to come from the President's convoy.

He managed to drag himself into a deserted house. The windows were shattered, the front door was hanging on one hinge, and the house had already been looted. The pantry was empty, but he found a bottle of water in the footwell of one of the cars in the garage. He swallowed four aspirin from his small personal first aid kit that hung from his vest, and then he checked his tablet and was very pleased to find out that it could connect with one of the surviving MILSTAT birds. He sent a message to Captain Miller: "Bird shot down by MANPAD at the entrance to the mine. Crashed two miles from mine. Hiding in house, 1827 Wood Hallow. White, burn marks, facing the city. Both pilots are dead, I'm injured; most likely broken ribs and left wrist."

Rand was very happy when the tablet quickly lit up with the answer, "Roger, sent message to Master Sergeant Crocket, he is closer to you and better experienced at getting people to safety. Will hit you back ASAP as he responds."

Crockett shook his head. "That major gets into more trouble than any other officer I know." He called his team together. "Listen up! We've been tasked with pulling Major Rand's nuts out of the fire. The poor SOB had the SecDoD's copter shot down. I don't know if we should save him because the Secretary is going to rip him to shreds when we're done. We'll have to continue the hunt for Letts afterward, so listen good: he was overflying the entrance to the mines under Kansas when a MANPAD took his bird down. I don't know where they got SAMs, but we can guess they might have more of them, so let's be very careful. We're going to have to tear up the freeway to reach him before the people holding the mines locate him. Load up, we leave in five minutes."

At the entrance to the mines, a general in a pressed uniform asked the two soldiers on guard duty, "Did you hit it?"

The first soldier shook his head. "Sir, mine went after a decoy and missed them."

The general shot the soldier between his eyes. "And you?"

"Sir, mine struck the Blackhawk and brought it down in the woods. You can see the smoke where it went down. I am still here because I didn't want to leave my post and leave us vulnerable."

"Corporal, did you hear the private? He understood his position, and he shot down the snooping Blackhawk. Then he called me with the news and picked up his rifle to defend his position. He's a good soldier, while you're a poor excuse for a corporal." A single bullet that struck the corporal between his eyes ended his life before his body struck the ground. "Private, take the chevrons from the corporal and put them on. You have done real good."

The newly minted Corporal smiled and saluted the general. "Corporal, I want you to take four more people and locate the crash site. If there are any survivors, bring them here. If any are too wounded to make it here, put them out of their misery. Bring me every scrap of paper and computer you find."

"Yes, sir."

Rand knew he couldn't hold his M7 with a broken left wrist, but that didn't stop him from using the corner of the window frame as support so he could use his right hand to pull the trigger. He was glad his rifle was equipped with a suppressor that, combined with subsonic ammo, made the rifle sound like a soft 22. His 4X scope showed him five people searching for the crash site. He thought he might be lucky in that they might not realize there had been a passenger and thus not search for him.

The corporal, pleased with the General's attention and his new rank, studied the crashed Blackhawk. "Why were they overflying our base? They didn't have any externally mounted rockets or even a machine gun. I wonder if they had a passenger. I want everyone to walk in increasingly larger circles searching for signs of a survivor."

Rand watched the soldiers. *Hmm, Army ACU uniforms. They're wearing the latest helmets, they have M16s or M4s, and their side arms are the older Beretta pistols. They have been taken from the Guard. I don't remember an Army base in Kansas City. I don't know how much combat they saw if any in the sandbox. Oh shit, one is a hunter, and he's picked up my trail. All it took was some drops of blood and broken plants for him to follow me. I looked behind me when I reached the subdivision, and I didn't notice any blood so my trail should stop at the end of the woods. I walked down driveways so I wouldn't leave boot prints in the damp grass.*

Rand pulled the barrow back from the window, he used a hand-held mirror, he'd discovered on the dresser in the master bedroom. *Hmmm, they lost my trail. They don't have enough people or time to check every house, so it looks like they're going to check the row closest to the woods. They assumed I'd pick the closest house. Wrong again buddy. I'm not completely stupid.* Rand watched them march back into the woods empty-handed. *I wonder what they're going to report. They had a good trail that ended fifty yards from the end of the woods. I bet they never mention it and just assume that whoever I am, I'm already gone. I hope Crockett gets here soon; those aspirins didn't do crap for me.*

Crockett's vehicles were very quiet. He sat on a hill watching the soldiers search   for   Major   Rand. "Corporal, bring me the sniper rifle. The big one."

Crockett made sure the suppressor was tightly screwed in. "527 yards. Here goes a nice 50 caliber. Hope you enjoy it," he whispered to the standing corporal who was watching for anyone who might surprise them. He had a fifth sense when trouble was close, and that's why Crockett liked having him around. The 26" barrel softly barked as the 647-gr bullet left the barrel at 3,000 Fps. (The same as the M16 firing a 55-gr bullet.) The bullet fired by the corporal standing next to Crockett struck the trooper to the left. The corporal had sighted the soldier on the right with his 308, firing a 178-gr bullet at 2,400 Fps. The soldier Crockett targeted didn't feel a thing as his head exploded. The soldier on the right was hit in his chest. His heart exploded from the pressure in his chest as the heavy-weight bullet entered the chest cavity.

Crockett smiled. "Good shot. Continue working from the right to the center, and I'll go from the left to the center. The one who reaches the center wins a beer."

"Deal."

In less than a minute, all five, including the newly minted corporal were dead. Crockett whispered, "Install the thermal scope and scan the area so we can locate any who may be hiding. They can't hide their temperature from the thermal scope."

"Sarge, clean, nothing else is around."

"Good, let's go find our wayward Major and get out of here before more nosey soldiers show up."

Chapter 14

Rand watched the soldiers searching for him fall as if they'd been hit by a sledgehammer. Each of the bodies were left with bloody holes where the bullets had entered. The .308 JHP bullets expanded on entry, transferring three times more energy into the target than the old 5.56 mm M 16/4 rounds.

Rand found a white tablecloth in the dining room; he tied it around the barrel of his rifle and waved it out of the shattered dining room window. He hoped his rescuers would see it and not shoot at him through the house's thin walls.

He heard a familiar voice, but he couldn't immediately place it. "You with the white flag, or should I call it what it is: a white tablecloth. Come out with your hands above your head and leave the rifle behind."

Rand yelled back, "I have a broken wrist and broken ribs. I was in a plane crash."

"No, you were in a helicopter crash, weren't you Major?"

"You know who I am?"

"Of course, I do, Major. I was asked – no I believe the appropriate term is *ordered.* – to come and retrieve your ass. I was getting close to Letts' base when I received the *order* to find you and make sure you were returned to your convoy. They also told me to return the Secretary's helicopter in one piece. We found what's left of the helicopter already; the Secretary is going to be mighty pissed. That bird is like Humpy Dumpty, it ain't going to be put back together again. When you screw up, you really do it royally. Come out so we can get you some medical help."

"I'm coming. I'm slow and in a lot of pain. In case you're curious, both pilots died in the crash when a large tree branch came through the windshield. It tore them apart. I didn't have the time to bury them. Soldiers from what I assume was the tunnel were searching for survivors. They were the ones who fired the MANPAD that knocked us down."

"Yeah, we found them, and I had them buried. I have their dog tags. I figured you broke something. I'll send two men in to help you. Please do me a favor and don't shoot them."

Rand laughed, finally matching the voice to a face and realizing he'd been speaking with Crockett. He wondered how Crockett and his team had managed to locate him so quickly, but he knew this is what they did.

Two of the Delta Operatives helped Rand walk out of the deserted house. Crockett told his men to take him to site X and wait for a pickup. Rand had no idea where or what site X was.

As far as the pickup goes, he thought it might be a C-130 that would use the freeway as a runway. He was taken to a parking lot in front of a burned-out strip mall. There were imprints of people burned into the bricks from the thermal pulse the Russian nukes had shot like a wave from ground zero. The asphalt parking lot had literally melted and reformed into waves.

There were two dozen skeletons of burned cars. Their interiors were charred, as were a handful of people who had had the misfortune of being in the wrong place at the wrong time. They had been too close to ground zero when the bomb hit. Rand had never seen people whose skin had melted like taffy before. He already knew he'd have nightmares for months.

One of the Delta Operators had bandaged Rand's wrist and ribs. "Major, the only thing I can do for your ribs is to wrap them. You'll be very sore for a while, but shit happens. You're still among us. I'm sure Captain Gold is going to be happy if there's anything left of her mind."

"She'll be fine. She came around just as I was leaving, and she recognized me."

"Major, funny thing about strokes, she might be okay for a while and then fall back to not remembering anything."

"She's strong; she will recover."

"For your sake, I hope you're right."

Rand looked up as the muffled sound of a strange helicopter was flaring and landing next to him. "What is that? It doesn't look like any Blackhawk I've ever seen."

Crockett smiled and waved at the pilot. That's one of ours: quiet and almost invisible to radar. We use it to get in and out of places we don't want to be discovered in. It's going to take you to your convoy. Your doc can check you over; he'll most likely put a cast on your wrist and check my wrappings on your ribs. We'll be here waiting for you. We have to figure out who the general running this place is. We'll do a little recon for you so you'll have a good idea what you're up against."

Rand nodded and looked at Crockett. "Did you see their uniforms? I bet they were in the Guard."

"I did. We cut their dog tags off and will find out who they were. I have a bad feeling about these mines."

Rand winced in pain as he was belted into the helicopter. "I thought we'd find some families who took shelter in the mines, not another Warlord."

"I have some more bad news for you to tell the Secretary."

"Hit me, no, let me reword that: please don't hit me. Why do you want me to forward a message for you? I thought you guys were fearless."

"You're an officer and his golden boy. I'm a simple Master Sergeant."

"That's not the way I heard people speak about you. What's the story?"

"We discovered some notes indicating that Letts has been communicating with other Warlords."

"Yeah, I see why you don't want to deliver it yourself. You don't want the mission of locating all of these Warlords and putting them in the ground."

"See, for an officer, and especially a Major, you're pretty smart."

"Wow, that's the nicest thing you've ever said to me."

"Major, I don't like AARs or any report. As a Major, you live for paperwork, so do me this solid, and I'll owe you one."

"Deal. I'll pass your message on. He's going to ask me if you have a list of the ones she's been chatting with. Is she planning on taking over the country?"

"Nope. I don't have a list. I do know they've been talking about how to break up the country so each operates a sizable portion of it. The last thing they want is for us to put the country back together. They're going to do everything they can to stop us from succeeding."

"I can see that. Work on that list. We both know he's going to ask me a shit load of follow-up questions that I won't be able to answer."

"Okay, I'll try to get them to you before you retire for the night. By the way, if I were you, I'd triple the guards around your base camp."

"Good idea. Do you know anything about them hitting us?"

"No hard information, but it's what I'd do if I were in their shoes."

"Now that you mentioned it, I agree. If I had the people, I'd do it too."

Crockett closed the door. "Have a safe flight and give the Secretary my regards. Rand, one more item, you can not keep that bird, its one of four. It's mine."

"Master Sergeant, I'm sorry, I can't hear you." He leaned forward and waved goodbye to the Delta Operators from the front windshield.

Rand noticed that there weren't any windows to look out of, as he tried to come up with a good explanation for why the Secretary's bird was in a million little pieces and his personal pilots were dead. He also didn't relish telling him that the mines the President was planning on using as a location for the government were under the command of another Warlord. He silently prayed Gold was making progress. He held his chest; every breath hurt. He knew he was going to get an earful, and that he might even lose his company. He smiled to himself. *If they bounce me, I'll have a lot of time to spend helping Gold recover.*

He had a flash idea, and he called over to the pilot. "This craft is basically invisible to radar, right?"

"Major, why do I have a feeling you're going to suggest some foolish idea that's going to put us and this priceless bird at risk?"

"Captain, it's getting dark and there's no moon. We should be able to do a flyover of the tunnel and the entire city too. Turn the camera on, and we'll get some valuable information for the Secretary and the President. Maybe enough to keep me out of the shit hole I'm in for losing the Secretary's bird."

"Major, if we lose this bird, we'll be in crap so deep we'll never be able to crawl out of it. But what you suggest might be possible. Let me plot a course that will make us harder for their defenses to see. I'll make one pass, then we're out of here. I don't have sufficient fuel to waste. Hold on tight, this is going to be exciting."

There were two people standing on a small hill on each side of the opening to the mines. Each held a Stinger MANPAD on the ground by their feet. They didn't think anyone would be foolish enough to approach them by air after they had shot down a Blackhawk.

They heard the stealth helicopter when it was passing them, but by the time they'd lifted the launch tubes, they hadn't noticed the strange noise that prevented the thermal sensor in the nose of their Stinger missiles from locking onto anything. They turned the launch controls off and placed them back on the ground, one looked at the other, and then both shrugged their shoulders before falling to the ground with a small 22-caliber bullet embedded in their brains. The bullet had entered their heads between their eyes, and they were dead without being able to utter a sound. The bullets had been fired from a suppressed special rifle Delta snipers used to exterminate special pests.

Crockett told four of his people to silently enter the mines, gather as much intel as they could, and be back in an hour. He also asked two of his men to put on the two soldiers' jackets that their sniper had shot so anyone looking would believe they were seeing their own people. He told them to hold their Stingers on their shoulders in a ready position in case an officer stopped by and saw the launchers on the ground.

One of the men tasked with taking the place of the dead soldiers asked, "What do you want us to do if an officer does come snooping around?"

"Silently kill him before he sounds the alarm, then toss his body in the gully with the other two."

Chapter 15

Abdullah Mohammed was the mayor of Alton Illinois which had a large population of Muslims. They had been settled there by Presidents Obama and Biden. Obama had settled large groups of Muslims in 'Middle America' hoping they would spread Islam throughout the country. There were already Muslim enclaves in both California and New York, but most of them had died in the war. There was also a large enclave in Minnesota.

Mohammed sent messengers on motorcycles to announce that he was offering free homes to any Muslims who wanted to live in Southern Illinois where there were farms that supplied plenty of fresh food. The messengers found a small community in New York state who were very eager to leave, as the other survivors blamed the Muslims for the war. Indeed, they had already killed a third of the community.

It took three months for the Muslims from Minnesota and New York to arrive in Alton, and when they arrived, Mohammed welcomed them in. There were plenty of empty houses available after people had died in the war; many having simply given up and taken their own lives. The farmers in the area were literally begging people to help work the fields.

Alton quickly became the capital of what Mohammed called the foundation of the Caliphate. He pledged to expand Islam across the remains of the country. He told his followers the non-believers would be easy to convert because they had the two things they needed most: fresh food and clean water.

Mohammed sent messengers to the surrounding towns, spreading the word that Alton had plenty of fresh food and clean water since the town had several wells that tapped into underground streams.

The water was cool and clean. Large fires heated the water for tubs so people could bathe and get clean from their journeys.

The population quickly grew from a post-war number of 8,000 to 34,000. Alton was located on the shores of the Mississippi River, and the bridge that crossed it had been destroyed by floating debris. Containers, twenty-foot trailers, and even mobile homes had been in the pools of debris that rammed the bridge's supports. The supports weren't designed to absorb strikes to their foundations and the bridge had collapsed twenty-three days after the war. Mohammed knew that if he could get the bridge rebuilt, little Alton would become a key transportation hub in the future of the country. It might end up being the only way goods could cross the river.

While two fifths of the population, men and women, even kids from the age of ten to young adults working twelve hours a day, they had a workable plan to rebuild the bridge. One of the townspeople was a DMV engineer who drew up the plans to build a new bridge. Mohammed was pleased with the plans. He split the population into groups. One-fifth worked the fields with the farmers, and two-fifths trained to be soldiers. Mohammed planned to have everyone in his community above the age of ten trained. He knew it was only a matter of time before the new government wanted his bridge.

When a father of an eleven-year-old asked him why he was training the pre-teens, Mohammed smiled and replied, "They can handle small calibers, so they can scout for us. The Army won't expect children to be dangerous. We will use them to deploy mines to thin out our enemies."

"Great One, I mean no disrespect, but how do you know they will come here and attack us? We are a peaceful community of those who follow the words of Mohammed, blessings be upon him."

"I know the way their soldiers and officers think. Once they find out we rebuilt our bridge across the river, they will come. They will claim the bridge belongs to everyone and that it is necessary for the country, so they should guard it. They will allow anyone to cross, and they won't charge a toll. All we'll get for our hard work will be a thank you. I don't know about you, but I don't want the Army to interfere with our plans, and I don't want them settling other families, most likely Christians, among us. They don't follow the words of the Prophet. They don't accept the Prophet as a messenger from Allah. I am prepared to place my life, my very soul, in Allah's hands. I have to ask, are you also prepared to give your soul to Allah? Are your wife and children prepared?"

"Oh, mighty and holy one. I am sorry. I didn't think the results of our work would be desired by the non-believers."

"My friend, the sooner we complete the bridge, the sooner we will be the most powerful community in the country. If they want to get across the Mississippi, they will need our permission and that will cost them a pretty penny. A tax that will be shared among the faithful."

The father replied while bowing to the learned one, "As always you are correct. Truly Allah shines his love upon you." The father walked backward while still bent over as a sign of respect for their leader.

Mohammed told his closest advisors, "First we will take over the state south of Chicago that is a scorched dead zone. We'll let the Christians rebuild the city, and once they have, we'll move in and take it from them by force. I am going to send teams who will look like refuges into other communities; they will earn the trust of the people there, and after learning all they can, they'll kill the community leaders and promise the people food and even medical treatment if they join with us."

One of Mohammed's closest advisors shook his head. "Most honored sir, the Christians will pay lip service to converting, they will even learn the Prophet's words, but their hearts will remain tied to their Jesus, whom they believe is the son of their God."

"I agree with you. I don't expect them to convert. I will allow them to play their silly games until we're in a position to remove them. I project it will take us between six and eighteen months to totally control the state. Once we do, we'll repeat the plan in neighboring Ohio."

"Holy One, why not Iowa first?"

"They are too conservative and will fight and die before they even pay us lip service to convert. I want to establish a strong Caliphate and not spill useless blood until we are strong enough to destroy all of our enemies. We will conquer Illinois, Ohio, Minnesota, and Michigan. Once we meld the people in those states into loyal followers of the Prophet, we can turn our heads to other areas. One area in particular I have my eye on is the mines under Kansas City. Think of an underground city that needs no heat or cooling. Deep enough to survive a nuclear strike. That will be our seat of government because we will be safe and able to control who enters and exits."

His aides smiled and nodded their heads in agreement. Walking out of their leader's office one advisor whispered to another, "He is truly blessed by the Prophet. I for one, feel honored to serve one as great as he."

Mohammed was enjoying the company of his youngest wife who was thirteen. She hated him and what he did to her. There was a pounding on his door, but he knew his security would take care of whomever was disturbing his private time. His young wife was under the covers on their bed making him feel very relaxed when his security commander yelled through the closed bedroom door. "Holy One, there is a problem that needs your attention."

Mohammed swallowed hard as his bride pleased him. "Can it wait? I'm in the middle of something special."

"Holy One, I will wait in your office."

"Do that. I will be along soon."

He reached under the covers to stroke the blond hair of his bride. *We are going to have to dye that hair dark. I don't want people to think I took teens from their mothers. I can, I have the right to do so, but I need to be seen as the Holy One. OMG, that feels so good. Truly you are blessed.*

Mohammed's breath caught in his chest as his wife finished pleasing him. "Little one, go enjoy with my other wives. Something has come up that requires my attention. I don't have any idea how long I will be gone."

The young bride cried as she was escorted to her room. She handed her guard a note sealed with her wax seal. "Please deliver this to Abraham in the garage. His mother is ill; this is a note offering whatever we can to ease her suffering."

The guard silently nodded and took the note to the garage, where a sixteen-year-old was working on one of the master's Range Rovers. "Abraham, I have a note for you. I am sorry to hear about your mother. Do you think you should be with her if she is very ill?"

"I have to finish my work before I can leave to care for my dying mother. The Holy One requested I ensure this old Range Rover is ready for his use. I can't let the Holy One down. I have prayed to Allah to watch over my mother until I can return home."

The guard smiled and made a mental note to tell the Holy One how loyal this young mechanic was. The word from the guards and troops was that he was very gifted and could repair any of the thirty-year-old vehicles they were forced to use after the war.

The newer vehicles' computer chips had been fried by the massive EMP. He had even repaired his old Jeep, so it didn't stall every five minutes. The teen was a genius when it came to vehicles. The guard had learned the boy's father used to build what he called Hot Rods in their garage. Abraham had spent long cold and hot weekends and nights working at his father's side, who taught him everything he knew. The teen was blessed. The Holy One had let it be known that if any harm came to him, they would pray for death. A minute later, a very greasy teen with black hair and bright blue eyes pulled himself from under the Range Rover.

"Could you please do me a favor?"

"What can I do for the little mechanic?"

"Look how dirty I am. The Holy One likes his vehicles very clean. Could you sit behind the wheel and start it so I can tune it without getting the inside dirty?"

"Of course, I would be honored to."

"Thank you."

It took four attempts and then the old engine ran like a sewing machine. The guard knew the old Range Rover didn't previously run because he was one of the four that had pushed it into the garage. Two weeks later, it looked new and the engine ran as smooth as silk. "The paint looks so bright."

"I buffed and polished it. I found some old paint that was a very close match and I mixed it with some others I found to fill in some of the worst scratches. Do you think the Holy One will like it?"

"Like it? He will love it. He has to attend a meeting, so with your permission, I'll bring it to his house, and he'll know you worked a miracle on it."

"It wasn't a miracle. Allah guided my hands."

The guard didn't know there was a small tracking device mounted on the inside of the frame rails. It couldn't be seen and wouldn't be found unless they knew where to look. The guard was amazed at how the teen had turned a piece of junk into a smooth-running and gleaming SUV. When he reached Mohammad's house, the other guards came out to look at the SUV. One asked, "Is this the same junk we moved into the garage a couple of weeks ago?"

"Yup. It runs and looks like new. I think young Abraham must have worked around the clock. When I left him, he was covered head to toe in grease, oil, and paint. Even his hair was covered with it. He asked me to start it for him so he could tune it. I tell you that boy is a genius when it comes to cars and trucks."

All of the other guards agreed. While they were admiring the SUV, Mohammad was in his office listening to his chief of intelligence tell him, "Holy One, an American Blackhawk crashed at the mine under Kansas City."

"A real Blackhawk?"

"Yes, Holy One."

"Were there any survivors from the crash?"

"One. We saw a group of men and women quickly kill a platoon of soldiers who were searching for survivors. These people weren't in uniform, and they didn't miss a shot. They shot the soldiers with one or two to the chest and one to the head."

Mohammad thought, *Typical kill team shooting.* "Did you say they weren't wearing uniforms?"

"I did."

"Did you see what they drove?"

"Dirty, mud-caked pickups with machine guns mounted like ours."

Contractors. Someone very important was on that bird. I need to know who it was and why it was overflying the entrance to the mines. What do they know that I don't? Who could be important enough to send a squad of contractors? I didn't even know contractors still existed after the war. I had been told that any that survived were automatically drafted into the new Army. Something isn't adding up.

"Did our people notice if they found anyone alive?"

"Sir, we had three of our men hiding in the woods who were there on a routine scouting mission. Allah guided them so they were in the right position to see what was going on. The ones from the pickups killed the soldiers who were hunting the survivor. Our people retreated deeper into the woods to avoid being seen so we don't know what happened next."

"Didn't you say there were four soldiers hunting for the survivor and the ones from the pickups killed three? What happened to the fourth person?"

"We don't know. Our people said he gave a report to his officer and then disappeared."

Did he disappear or was he taken by these contractors? Something is happening at the mines; something I need to understand, because I had planned on making it our seat of government.

"Please see if your people can locate anything they may have left behind. I want you to send another team to learn what's happening at the mines."

"Yes, Holy One, I'll see to it myself."

The guard who was assigned to Abraham knocked after the intelligence officer had left. "Holy one, do you have a moment?"

"Abuda, for you, all the time."

"Holy One, there is something outside I think you will enjoy seeing."

Mohammad was shocked at the condition of the SUV. "This is the same one we located a few weeks ago?"

"The very same. I watched young Abraham work on it every day."

"Does it run?"

"Holy One, like new. I drove it here from the garage."

"Come, we must take this for a ride." An hour later they returned, and Mohammad was smiling from ear to ear. "I love it. We must reward him for his hard work. Tell him he can select one of my haram girls for a long weekend. When he does, I don't want him bothered all weekend."

"Holy One, he mentioned that his mother is very ill. He was hoping to return home to care for her."

"No, I won't risk losing him. Send a team and a doctor to bring his mother here. I don't want to risk anything happening to our new chief mechanic. Bring him to me tomorrow for coffee. I want to tell him of his promotion and have his mother here at the same time. It will make a nice family reunion."

"Yes, Holy One."

Mohammad sat in his Range Rover, and he smelled the leather. *How did he get it to smell new? I have not smelled this scent in a year.* He tried to figure out who had control of the mines and why. That's when another aide told him, "Holy One, we have new information that the President is in a convoy. He's out of the protection the base provided for him."

"Do we know where he is going?"

"So far we don't know anything except that he's in a convoy."

"FIND OUT! If we can capture him, we will have a bargaining chip that could be exchanged for our Caliphate. We would win our battle without shedding any of our blood. We need to capture the President unharmed for him to be worth enough for them to agree to our terms."

The aide nodded.

"Am I clear?"

"Yes, Holy One."

Chapter 16

President McCarthy felt very relaxed sitting in the rear of his up-armored SUV. The rear compartment usually carried six people, but today it was only the President and myself. The soundproof and bulletproof internal barrier was in its up position so the driver and the security officer sitting shotgun next to him couldn't overhear us.

I pointed to the electronic map on my tablet. "Mr. President, according to this map we will enter Indian—"

"Native American."

I nodded my understanding. "We'll be entering the Native American states in one hour. Do you know what you're going to say when they ask for our destination?"

"I don't want to lie to them, but on the other hand, I don't want to broadcast our destination so that spies for that SOB of a Warlord Letts learn of our plans."

I slowly nodded. "Mr. President, once we turn north toward our destination, it will no longer be a secret. I'm hoping that Major Rand discovers every ambush and terminates whoever set it up before we reach them."

McCarthy tilted his head. "I understood the route had been cleared, and we faced no threat."

I looked into the eyes of the president and the man I now called friend. "I made no such statement. Even if Rand locates a site and kills them, others will probably take their position. There is no law and order in the 'Bad Lands.'"

"Bad Lands? That's a new one. Who named the central states that?"

"I really don't recall. It seems to have happened around three weeks ago. Someone on my staff just called the area the Bad Lands, and within a couple of days, everyone on my staff called them that. It suits the area though, as the only law and order there is whatever the Warlords supply. Some run their areas with an even hand, and others rule as if they were kings. Some have even brought back the old rule of *jus primae noctis*."

McCarthy shook his head in disgust. "Are you telling me they reverted to rules from the Middle Ages? If I remember my Latin correctly, that means, the Law of the First Night. Where the Lord takes every virgin bride on her first night."

"That's correct. There are also stories that if a family can't pay their taxes, their sons and daughters are taken as slaves."

McCarthy got angry. "Slaves!? We have slavers in America? When did this happen?"

"Shortly, and I mean almost immediately after the last nuke exploded on our country. The rise of these Warlords led to the reintroduction of slave labor. With the exception of gold and silver, there wasn't any currency. Paper money didn't even make good toilet paper because it wasn't paper. Its value was based on the faith people had in the Federal Government being able to stand behind it and agree that it had value. Without a working government the dollar bills were useless. Well, not completely useless, I suppose, as I heard some people did use them as fire starters. They burn hot enough to light damp wood."

McCarthy looked shocked. "You're pulling my leg, aren't you?"

"Why would I lie to you? No one has any faith in the dollar anymore, and if you were in their shoes, perhaps you'd think the same. These are people who lost everything, who lost family members, who watched everything they owned get destroyed. The things they've seen and lived through would turn your stomach. You've been shielded from seeing the hell our people have to live with. You will see their suffering on this trip."

"What can we do for them?"

"You need to get the government back on its feet, take a stand, and give a powerful speech condemning the Warlords and their slavery. Tell the people help IS coming. Tell them food will be delivered very soon. We should stop at every farm and find out what they need to increase their production and transportation so we can feed our people."

"General, how can I tell people that food is on the way when we don't even control the warehouses where the hundreds of thousands of MREs are stocked? How can I promise them anything?"

"Then tell them the truth. All of the truth. They can handle the truth if they know it IS the truth."

"You want me to tell them everything?"

"Everything that impacts them. Tell them we need their help to cross the Mississippi. We have some good news. I just received a run of images from one of our remaining birds, it appears someone in Alton is working on repairing their bridge that crosses the Mississippi."

McCarthy sat up, his eyes showing his excitement. "Someone is repairing a bridge across the Mississippi. What can we do to assist them? Is it along the way to Kansas City?"

I hid my smile, I knew McCarthy would jump at the chance to get a bridge, any bridge, across the river. "We can send them a couple of squads of Seabees and one from the Army Corp of Engineers."

"I like it. Send as many people as you can spare and whatever materials they need."

"Sir, the question of ownership is going to come up."

"Why would they believe they owned it?"

"Because it starts in their town, and they drew up the plans and are supplying the manpower and building materials."

"If they own it, won't they then be able to charge tolls to use it?"

"I was going to mention that..."

"You were going to mention that when? How long will it take them to complete the bridge?"

"That I honestly can't answer. The few overhead images we have, show the beginnings of a bridge that won't support trucks; the crossings would have to be done on foot or by bicycle or motorcycle. There aren't many running trucks or cars operating in the nation, and most of them are what would have been considered classic cars. Those built before computers controlled the engines."

McCarthy looked out of the window. "We need working trucks and cars if we're going to rebuild the country. What can we do to repair enough vehicles to provide mobility?"

I looked at McCarthy and I chose my words wisely. "If we supply thousands of vehicles, we will be enabling the Warlords to attack further from their bases of operation. We will be enabling our enemies to strike us."

"What do you suggest? I assume you have another idea?"

"I do. We first have to defeat the Warlords, and then we have to feed our hungry and supply basic medical treatment. Right now, the old wild west was more livable than most of the country is today. People are dying every day from infections that would have been treated with antibiotics before the war. People have to live with broken bones, old children's diseases are making a comeback, and cancers from the radiation are spreading like wildfire. I could continue... You've been focused on rebuilding the government, but you should focus on taking care of the people. Leave the rebuilding capital to us. We have companies from the Army Corp of Engineers, Navy Seabees, and FEMA construction teams. Let us provide security and the rebuilding. Without a lot of EPA reports required we can move very quickly.

"I've recently received a report that a Warlord has already taken over the mines and is using them as his headquarters. I urged you not to move too quickly. We have to clear the route, the highwaymen and thieves move back in as quickly as we clear them out. We also need to complete a detailed recon of the mines so we know what we're walking into."

The President slowly nodded his head, "Is that why we're moving so slowly?"

"We're moving slowly because I'm trying to protect you and what's left of our federal government. If we lose to the Warlords, there won't be any freedoms, and there won't be any America. We'll be in the new Dark Ages. One we may never climb out of. There won't be an Industrial Revolution to change people's lives. The Warlords will want to keep their people poor and afraid of them. You represent the light that will be needed to destroy the darkness that has covered our country."

"I hear you. What are your plans?"

"You're going to get a tour of the country you're the president of, and then you're going to bring the light that will pierce the dark. You will demonstrate to the people that you will tend to their needs. You're going to give them food and set up MASH units to provide basic medical treatment. You've been so focused on rebuilding the government that you lost sight of what really matters. You're going to promise the people security. You're going to promise them running water and electricity in a year."

McCarthy asked, "Just how do you think I'm going to feed everyone? I'm not Jesus. I can't feed everyone with a loaf of bread and a fish. How am I supposed to make the water run?"

"We're going to help the people in Alton finish their bridge, and then we're going to use it to cross the Mississippi and take the hundreds of thousands of MREs stored in the mines in Indiana. I have been establishing FOBs, really forts like we did when we moved west, they are being established along the route to Kansas City to act as safe havens. I have been planning on how to save the best of America and cut out what weakens us. We'll cut the cancer out."

"You're sounding like a politician. Where are you getting the people to do all of this?"

I smiled, "Three Marine MEIs will dock in Mayport in a week. We're getting hundreds of walk ins to our forts and to the existing bases every day. We're rebuilding the military along the lines of the Marines, everyone is a rifleman..."

"Rifleperson."

"Sorry, everyone is first a rifleperson. They are being retrained to be quick and deadly. We have more weapons than we could ever use. I have air force teams checking the planes stored in the desert. Soon, we'll have an air force again."

"Don't you worry about China?"

"I hope they got the message, if they didn't, then we'll give them another dose of Trident."

"I picked the right person to be my partner."

"Don't go there, I'm not a politician. No thanks, I'll leave that to you. I have zero patience for what you do. I'll get you to the mines, and clear the country of the outlaws. You focus on building a new government, one that represents the people, all of the people. I suggest you also promise the people a new census and elections in two years."

*****

One of Letts' intelligence officers entered her office with a huge grin on his face. "Ma'am, we have figured out where McCarthy is going."

"Don't keep this to yourself. Where is he going? If we can take him out, the military may fall apart and thus enable us to keep what we've taken without a fight."

"Ma'am, he is in one of three convoys going to the mines under Kansas City. We received the information from one of our people who works for the acting Secretary of State."

"Can you show me on the wall map their route and where they are currently?"

*****

At that exact moment, hundreds of miles from Letts' headquarters, an aide knocked on Mohammad's office door with the same information. Mohammad yelled to his security officer, "Assemble a strike team of our best people. We're going to capture and hold for ransom the President."

"Yes, Holy One. Do you think we should go in the technicals or use the old cars?"

"He is bound to have an armed escort, so we'll take the technicals with the largest machine guns. I also want to bring a dozen RPGs in case we have to blow up his escort vehicles. I will assume they are armored so we'll be prepared to destroy them. Let's leave in fifteen minutes."

"Holy One, it will take us longer to pull the teams together."

"If it does, the first one I shoot will be you."

The two Warlords left within minutes of each other, but Mohammad had the longer trip ahead of him. He didn't want to miss what he thought was going to be an excellent spot for an ambush.

He reminded everyone not to shoot the President; they could kill anyone else, if there were any women in the convoy, they could have them, but if anyone shot the President they would pray for death.

Letts told her people to capture the President and as many in his party as possible, "The more of his people we capture, the more of them we will have to torture in front of the President. He will break as soon as one of his women staffers begs for her life. Remember, don't hit the President. We'll lay rows of spike strips in front, behind, and along the shoulder of the freeway where we will ambush the convoy. Hurry, I don't want to miss our best opportunity to capture him and bring our dreams to reality in one fall swoop."

Unknown to both Warlords, they had each selected the same blind corner in front of a rest stop that was hidden from the main road because it was set lower than the surface as their ambush site. The President's convoy was slowly moving through Texas. They stopped at almost every small town so the President could see with his own eyes the misery suffered by his citizens. An armed escort ensured the Texas Rangers kept their distance.

What both Warlords also didn't know was that the captain of the Texas Rangers planned on ambushing the President too, so the governor could reach an agreement for Texas to leave the union and form their own country. He too had decided on the same blind curve as the Warlords. The next morning was going to be very interesting, with two Warlords and the Captain of the Rangers hoping to dig in and set up an ambush in the exact same place.

Chapter 17

Captain Gold opened her eyes and looked around her room. Most of it looked familiar, but in many ways, different too. She tried to remember what was different, but her mind was cloudy. She couldn't focus. No matter how much she tried to concentrate on the details of the room, she couldn't make them match. It was like that game of comparison between two pictures where one was different in minor details than the other. She used to enjoy that game and she could usually quickly see the differences. Now it was as if her mind was playing games on her instead. She couldn't figure out what was real and was an illusion.

When the nurse entered her room with her breakfast, she refused to touch the food because she knew it wasn't real. She didn't answer any of the nurse's questions because she knew the nurse wasn't real either. Gold closed her eyes and napped, believing that when she opened them again, everything would be back to normal, and the illusion of the nurse would disappear. She thought she would be in her uniform and commanding her company. Internality, she smiled, remembering she reported to her lover, Major Rand. They'd agreed to play by the rules until the mission was completed. Then, they would meet with the Secretary of Defense and ask for permission to marry. She knew she might have to resign her commission, but being with Rand would be worth it.

When Gold opened her eyes for the third time that morning, she saw a doctor standing next to her bed, and she forced herself to focus on him. She thought, *they sent Doctor Josef Mengele, the Nazi doctor from the Auschwitz extermination camp and he wants to run his evil experiments on me. I won't let him touch me. I'll die before I allow him to learn my secrets. I've been trained in escape and avoidance. They're not going to use their dirty tricks on me, and I won't let them perform any of their experimental surgeries on me, either.*

The fools didn't even restrain me. They thought I was too weak from their drugs, but they made a huge mistake. I need to get a set of their scrubs and badges so I can be taken for one of them and make my escape. No one will pay me any attention. I'll be able to walk out of this place. Once I'm in the parking lot, it will be easy to steal a car, and I'll be gone. Once I'm out of here, I'll find our lines, and they'll protect me. When I tell them the Jews didn't capture and kill Mengele, I can tell our people where he is. I'll be remembered forever as the person who got the Nazi devil. His evil experiments must have taught him how to stay young.

I'm a trained American soldier, an officer, trained to lead soldiers into combat. I aced all of the tests to become one of only a hand full of women who qualified as a Ranger. I know what I have to do, and I'm ready to do it. Whatever drugs they've been pumping into me to get me to talk are a waste of time; I'll never talk. I'm going to spill coffee on the next nurse who comes in here and I'll ask her how far she has to go to change uniforms. When they give me my night pills, I'm going to hold them in my cheeks like a squire, and I'll pretend to sleep till 0300.

I'll put my pillow and a rolled up blanket under the covers so it looks like I was sleeping. Anyone checking from the door will see the lump under the covers and assume it's me. I noticed they leave the doors unlocked, and the lights aren't keyed to the doors. Last night, they didn't wake me to check my vitals, so I'm guessing they stopped doing that. That will give me until the morning team arrives at 0700 to check on me. I can get far away from this prison in four hours.

I'll need a badge to open the doors without being stopped. Most people only glance to make sure a badge is being worn, but they don't check if the picture matches the wearer. There's no moon tonight and it may rain so it will be cloudy and dark making tonight the perfect night to escape. At 10:00 Gold's night nurse said this was the last time she would be in to check her vitals unless the monitors reported something was wrong.

"Try to get some sleep, it will help you. Your body can heal itself if it gets enough rest. I won't let anyone bother you until breakfast. Do you need anything?"

I wanted to say, yes, I need a badge, a set of scrubs and a car. But I said, "Thank you. I have a lot of trouble getting back to sleep after being woken up." *I put my head down, then I had another idea.*

Gold thought for a moment and said, "Nurse, is it possible to unplug the monitors just for the night? I toss and turn, and they get pulled, then the alarm goes off, then you have to come in to see if I'm okay when you know I'm fine and that I either just rolled or had to use the bathroom."

"You're doing a marvelous job recovering, I don't see any issue with not hooking you in at night. All of your vitals are normal."

"Thank you so much." *Step one checked off.*

"I need you to take your night pills." The nurse knew they included a sleeping pill, so she wasn't very concerned about Gold wandering the halls.

"Sure. And can I please have some cool water in my pitcher for tonight, in case I get thirsty?"

"Sure, I'll be right back." Gold waited till the nurse left her room, then she spat the pills out into a tissue she hid in her bed. When the nurse came back, she knocked a cup of decaf coffee onto her. "I'm so sorry," she said.

The nurse smiled. "It's not a problem, the spare uniforms are only three doors down and it happens at least once a shift. I'll be right back."

Gold smiled. *Step two check.*

The nurse returned and said, "Please open your mouth. I need to check that you swallowed your pills."

Gold opened her mouth, then the nurse said, "Good night, Captain, sleep tight."

"Good night, Nurse Wells. I appreciate everything you do for me."

Nurse Wells smiled, turned the lights off, and closed Gold's door, and Gold laid down and pretended to sleep. *I might as well get a little sleep; 0300 will be here before I know it. I'll set my internal clock to wake me. I've always been able to wake when I wanted or needed to.*

Gold opened her eyes at 0255. *Right on time.* She listened for any footsteps. *At nighttime, the footsteps echo, unlike during the day when the background noise masks it. I don't hear anything. I'll set up my bed so anyone looking in will think I'm sleeping.*

Gold slipped out of bed and cracked the door; she couldn't see anyone moving. She assumed the nurses were hanging out at the nurse's station that was on the other side of the wing. She couldn't see them, and they wouldn't be able to see her moving around either. If she got caught, she planned on saying that she didn't know where she was, so the nurse would assume she had been sleepwalking.

She found the supply room. It was right where Nurse Wells had said it was, three doors down. She noticed the rooms between hers and the supply room were empty. She thought, *even better they won't be called to come down here. How nice they label the supply room, and it doesn't have a lock on the door.* Minutes later, she walked out of the supply room in a clean, starched nurse's uniform and white shoes. *I still need an ID.* She passed a door marked 'locker rooms, staff only.' The door wasn't locked, and it didn't even have a lock on it. She gently pushed the door open and entered the room that was filled with lockers. She remembered her training in how to pick these locks. After opening four lockers, she hit paydirt. An ID for someone who looked a little like her was hanging in the locker as was a printout of their work schedules.

Gold realized that the ID badge had to be a spare one, because according to the schedule, the nurse, Ms. Welling, was working. Either that, or she had forgotten to attach the badge to her uniform. Gold saw a small purse on the floor of the locker. *Car keys, twenty dollars in cash, plus a couple of dollars in change, and lordly, look at this: a cell phone. The key fob has a large "H" on it, it's for a Honda. That will make my search easier. It narrows my search down.*

Gold slipped out of the locker room, stood tall, and grabbed a clipboard from a rack outside of a patient's room. She walked like she belonged there. She slowly walked into the parking lot and realized she didn't know which car was the nurse's, so she clicked the remote and saw a dark gray Honda Civic that flashed its lights. *Great color to make a run with. I'll slowly pull out with the lights off. If I have to, I'll pull the fuse so the damn daylight lights don't come on.*

Fifteen minutes later, Gold had pulled into an apartment parking lot. She searched for another Civic to swap license plates with. The fifth car she saw was a black Civic. *Gray, black, most can't tell the difference at night. I'll swap plates just before dawn. I don't think anyone has the ability to even check plates anymore, but when the nurse reports her car stolen, she will give the plate number to the army, this way, they most likely won't stop me since the plate won't match what they're looking for.*

Ten minutes later, Gold had pulled the GPS fuse so the car couldn't be easily tracked, she knew most of the GPS birds had been destroyed by Russian anti-satellite weapons, but she didn't want to take any chances the Nazis could locate her. As the sun began turning the eastern sky pink, she swapped the plates for the third time and got lucky, because she found two Civics parked side by side. She took the front plates off of both cars, one to swap onto her car, and she kept the second as a spare set that she planned to change later in the day.

She put a mask on her face so any cameras couldn't get a good image of her, and she also removed the ID badge so the camera couldn't take a picture of it and use it to locate her. She used the restroom at an all-night waffle house twenty miles from the VA hospital on the base in Arizona she'd been flown to, she discovered a chip in the ID badge, which she submerged in water, hoping to short it out. She used the twenty dollars to buy her breakfast and coffee to go. The mask, combined with her head held down, made sure that cameras couldn't get a clean image of her. She also wore a pair of rubber gloves she'd taken from her room. That way she didn't leave her fingerprints anywhere. No one paid any attention to the gloves or mask. This was America after the nuclear war. Many people suffered burns they were ashamed of and had respiratory issues from the smoke and debris in the air.

Gold had been driving due east, but she now changed her direction to the north with a plan to enter Utah, then east to Colorado, where she intended to hide till the heat of her disappearance cooled down. She didn't want to cross Indian lands. She knew they had border crossings and exchanged data with the new DHS. She hoped she could find a way to call Rand. She had left the cell phone at the Waffle House in the outside trash container, anyone who found it would lead them to believe she was driving due east.

The roads were still empty of civilian cars, and she didn't want to stand out and risk getting stopped by the police, or military patrols so she drove slowly, a couple of MPH under the posted speed limit if such things even existed any longer.

As the sun broke through the clouds, Gold decided she needed a place to get some sleep and hide. She turned into what looked like an empty subdivision, and she thought, *most likely the owners fled or died when the clouds of fallout from California arrived. I don't see anyone outside. All of the homes look empty. I'll find one with an empty garage and pull the car in, grab a few hours of sleep, and then plot my next move. So far, my plan has been a complete success. The broken phone will most likely send them on a search due east. Maybe I can keep them off my tail long enough to hook up with the Major. He's the one person I know can trust.*

She checked houses that were located three streets into the subdivision, so she was away from the main street that ran along the front row of houses. She had only seen a few trucks on the roads since she'd broken out of the hospital. She realized some cars and trucks weren't affected by the EMP as badly as people thought they would be. Many cars had their computers shielded or were inside garages when the nukes exploded. She guessed the EMP wasn't as severe as most thought it would be.

Gold pulled up to a rare house that still had its windows intact, and with the garage door unlocked, she pulled in next to a 1964 Ford Falcon. The house was empty, and she had to break in because the door between the garage and the main house was locked. She'd found a toolset that allowed her to break the mounting and gain access to the bolt head. Once in the house, she was surprised to find that it was neat, and the pantry was still full of canned food. The power was off, but the water was running. She didn't understand why, but she was happy. She found the water heater in the garage. The house owners had turned it off, and as she turned it on, she realized that the gas was still flowing, so she lit the pilot light and dreamed of a hot shower.

She emptied some cans of chicken noddle soup into a pot and heated it on the gas stove, *Biden would have been pissed that this house ran on gas.* She found a note on the fridge and understood why the gas worked: the house had a large propane tank buried in the backyard, one that had been fueled two days before the war. *I really lucked out. I bet this entire subdivision had propane tanks. I might chill out here for a couple of days.*

Gold enjoyed her soup and crackers that she found in the pantry, then she took a hot shower. She had looked at the pictures in the master bedroom and discovered that the house belonged to a single mother with two teens. *I wonder what happened to them. I'm glad they had triple-pane windows installed when they built the house. I don't want to do anything people driving or walking by would think abnormal. I'm going to hide out here for a couple of days. First, I'll take a nice nap.* She crashed on the king-sized bed in the master for six hours. When she woke up, she listened and couldn't hear any sounds. *It's so quiet. I'm not used to it being this quiet. I don't think anyone will find me here. I've changed the plates three times and used three different states' plates. I know there isn't anyone there to tell the police who owns the plates anyway.*

I have food, cases of bottled water in the garage, hot water, and a very comfortable bed. I wonder how long it will be before the heat on my breaking out cools down.

At 7 a.m., Gold's two nurses from the night and day shifts entered her room to check on her. The night nurse wanted to introduce the day nurse to her. The day nurse carried Gold's breakfast tray while the night nurse carried the pot of what passed for coffee in the hospital.

The night nurse placed the coffee on the side table as the day nurse placed the tray on it next to the pot. The night nurse tapped the lump in the bed while saying, "She sometimes sleeps very deeply, it's the sleeping meds the doctor has her on. He's hoping the sleep will help her to recover."

"Come on sleepy head, it's time for you to wake. I have a new nurse I want to introduce you to."

The day nurse frowned. "I don't think that's her. It feels like a pillow; maybe two of them. My kids sometimes pull that stunt on me."

The night nurse pulled the covers back and shook her head. "Shit. I'm screwed. I agreed to stop checking on her because she said it was hard for her to get to sleep. You better call security."

At the same time, another nurse was thinking that she had lost her car keys and was going to have to check with lost and found to see if anyone had found them. A moment later she heard, "Attention, silver alert, silver alert. All staff check with your stations for a silver alert."

The missing person had been named a silver alert because their wandering-off patients were senior vets suffering from various memory issues. The nurse with the missing keys shrugged her shoulders and reported to her station. She learned that Captain Gold was missing. That's when she mentioned that her car keys were also missing. Security quickly questioned the nurse. "Was anything else missing?"

"Let me check, yes, twenty dollars and a handful of coins."

"What kind of car do you drive?"

"A blue 2001 Honda Civic."

"Do you remember the plates?"

"No. My registration was in the car."

"Okay, thank you."

"What about my car?"

"If we locate it, we'll let you know. Do you need a ride home?"

"I live on base. I can walk. Shit, my apartment keys were on my car keys. Do you think she's at my apartment?"

"Maybe, give us your address and we'll check it out."

Nurse Wells worried that something might happen to her. She had followed all of the VA's rules. Security grilled her for three hours before they were convinced, she wasn't part of Gold's escape plot. They also ordered every room checked to make sure she didn't escape with other patients. The commanding officer of the Army's Criminal Investigation Office, Colonel Guty wondered if Gold had been turned by Letts.

Days went by without any sighting of the blue Civic. Most of the cameras in the few remaining gas stations and restaurants had been out of order since the war. The colonel reached out to the Native Americans, who responded that they didn't have any record of a blue Civic passing through any of their border checkpoints. Guty had no idea where the captain might have gone. The Civic had an aftermarket head unit with GPS installed, but with most of the GPS birds destroyed in the war, there wasn't any way to track the car. Guty knew he had to report this to the Secretary because the captain was on a special list the Secretary wanted to be kept informed of. Guty knew this because he'd been included in the memo to the hospital in case the captain managed to slip out of the hospital.

Guty shook his head as he told his XO, "The fools knew she was on a watch list, and they let her go the night without checking on her. We have no idea when she left or where she went. They made it too easy for her. All we can do is issue an APB, but with so many people missing from the war, it will end up being someone's plate or TP. I'm going to have to tell the Secretary we lost her until she makes a mistake, and based on her background, I don't expect she's going to make a mistake."

"Sir, where would she go?"

"I have no idea, and according to the hospital staff, neither do they. It seems no one was interested in getting to know her that well, so she was allowed to slip right through their fingers."

"Sir, if you were her, where would you go?"

"Major, that's a very good question, and I don't have enough details about her to give you even a guess."

"I guess it's time to take my medicine and call the Secretary."

Chapter 18

I was furious, as I shouted, "Let me see if I understand this: you LOST Captain Gold. Am I correct!?"

Guty swallowed and replied, "Sir, it's not like we lost her. It's more like we can't find her."

"Colonel, the last I heard she was in the VA hospital at one of the most secure bases in the country, and then she disappeared from a locked room from a secured hospital with no transportation or clothes, and no money, and you can't find her. Am I still, correct?"

"Sir, she stole a car from one of the nurses. Her room wasn't locked, and we believe she managed to gain access to the supply room where the scrubs are stored. She could have worn a scrub and walked out of the hospital without anyone thinking differently. She would have fit right in."

"Her room wasn't locked? Maybe you don't understand what a high-value patient is or what my orders were. I thought they were very clear. Keep her under observation around the clock. I know I informed the hospital and your command that not only was she a high-value patient, but that she had been trained in how to escape and should be considered dangerous if she tried to do so. She was a Ranger for Christ's sake! Do you understand what a Ranger is? Do you understand how they're trained? If you had, you would have followed my orders and posted armed guards at her door and at the hospital's exits. How many hours was she missing before someone noticed she was gone?"

"Sir, we don't know. The night nurse was the last one to see her. That was at 2000, and no one entered her room again until 0700 when the nurse realized she was missing."

"I bet the captain would have waited until early morning when the night shift people were tired. She would have found a way to locate the supply room, and the locker room too. I bet she broke into some lockers to find the keys and some money, and once she had a car and was wearing scrubs, she could have gone anywhere, but she was trained in escaping from behind enemy lines.

"She was trained on how to survive off of the land. She excelled at the escape and hide courses. That training is part of her nature now, so I bet she's hiding out during the day and traveling at night. She would need a place to hide and access to food. She would also swap license plates. Have there been any reports of missing plates? I know plates aren't such a big thing today, but she would do it because it's part of her training."

"Sir, after the war there were enough thieves that no one cares about plates anymore. Wrong plates or no plates are in that category."

"I know that it is such a minor offense today that it is almost meaningless, but she wouldn't realize that as she would be operating purely on her training, and that would mean that she'll change plates and cars every couple of hours."

"Sir, with a car, she could be hundreds of miles away."

"I don't think so. She won't want to enter Native American territory. She would know they have a strict policy on people traveling through their state. I think she is still in the area. I bet she found an empty house, and she's hiding there waiting for things to cool down. She knows we don't have the manpower to search for her. I bet she'll surface in a week or two with different hair color and maybe even some tattoos to throw our facial recognition software off. Colonel, I'm not throwing rocks at you, but according to our records, you've never been in or led people in combat. Our Rangers are trained to escape enemy territory, and she passed that part of the test with flying colors. You're looking for an expert..."

"Sir, she's had a stroke, I don't think she remembers anything."

"Have you ever met the captain?"

"No, sir. I can't say that I have."

"Had you met her, you would have realized she remembers a lot more than you give her credit for. My expert on her told me she was making a miraculous recovery."

"Sir, you have an expert on Gold?"

"I do, and I plan to bring him back to find her."

"Sir, yes sir. I'll be happy to work with whomever your expert is."

"Colonel... in actuality, I should refer to you by your new rank: Captain. You didn't follow my orders, and I think you aren't the right person to lead the Military Police in our new nation. I'll be sending you new orders within the hour, and I promise you: you're going to learn a lot from your new assignment."

"My new assignment? What new assignment?"

"You're going to lead a squad, and I can safely promise you that *you will* see combat."

"General, I'm a cop, or at least I used to be one."

"Your record says you never drew your gun, and you almost missed the cut because you couldn't shoot straight. I saw your targets: you missed all of them. Your uncle, a captain in the force, made sure you kept your job. You're about to learn what the Army does on a day-to-day basis. We protect the Constitution and the citizens of America. Today our mission is to crush the various Warlords and their armies of fools."

"I was promised I'd never have to see combat when I signed on."

"Captain, that was then, and this is now. Everything changed when the first Russian missiles destroyed Washington."

A moment later a major entered the office. "Captain, I have been ordered to assume command of the Military Police forces. Oh, and I was told to tell you to leave the Eagles on the desk. By the way, here's your railroad tracks, please swap the Eagles with these."

"He doesn't waste any time, does he?"

"No, he doesn't. I met him on the return trip from Europe, not long after the Russians nuked our generals and our FOBs in Ukraine."

*****

Rand jumped out of the helicopter and was handed a secure envelope. "Sir, the Secretary ordered me to hand this to you the moment you landed. I'm to wait for your response."

"Shit. Let me see what he wants from me now."

Rand read the orders two times. "Damn it, does he already know I crashed his bird and is this my pound of flesh?"

"Sir, you're response."

"Sergeant, when I attended West Point, we were instructed that there were only three answers to any question. Those were: yes, sir, no, sir and the other one was: sir, no excuse, sir. Thus, my response is, 'Yes, sir.'" The Secretary outranks me, and he's given me a valid order, so I have to follow it."

"Sir, I was ordered to hand you this message slip if you agreed to follow the Secretary's orders.

Rand ripped open the sealed envelope and his face lost all of its color. "Sergeant, call that bird and tell the pilot he is return here to pick me up. Oh, and find some fuel for him; he's going to need it where we're going." Rand texted Captain Willis. "Drop everything and report to me."

Rand mentally pushed the helicopter to fly faster; he couldn't believe the message he'd received from the Secretary. Captain Gold had broken out of the VA hospital, and they had no idea where she was. Since he was the one person who was the closest to her, he was needed to help locate her. He sat in the stealth helicopter trying to figure out where she would have gone and why she ran. The last time he'd seen her, she was making a lot of progress. She recognized him and their times together. He thought she was making a recovery, but now he worried something had changed and the progress she'd made might have been reversed.

He realized that there must be something very important locked in her memory, something they needed to capture Warlord Letts, who was causing all sorts of problems in the surviving areas. She had raided every National Armory in four states. In two of them, she'd had to use torches to cut into the armories, and she'd been rewarded with racks of M4 automatic assault rifles, cases of hand grenades, LAWs rockets, and even Stinger shoulder-fired anti-aircraft missiles. In the back of the vault there were pallets of cases of ammo, and in the parking lot they had discovered working vehicles.

She had all the equipment and followers she needed to control her states and defeat the small American Army, but she didn't know that that small American Army was being boosted by walk-ins and returning units from Europe, Asia, and the Middle East. Most had been recalled and were on ships when the missiles flew over the North Pole, destroying Russia and most of America's cities. The returning units had followed their orders to report to the temporary bases established to welcome them: Marines, airmen and sailors alike.

The new units were ordered to restore order and defeat the Warlords. And when a general asked if it was legal for them to operate inside the CONUS, he was quickly told that the President had declared Martial Law, thus overriding the Posse Comitatus Act.

*****

Gold had spent three days in the house she'd taken over, and when the sun shined in and lit up the furniture on day three, she noticed that there was a covering of fine dust over everything. She thought it might be the deadly fallout she had learned about, but she remembered learning that most of the fallout would half-life down to a safe number within two weeks.

She decided three days in the same house was enough and it was time to move. She didn't want to use the Civic as it had been stolen, and the switching of the license plates wasn't going to help much without the national network. She thought that the Chevy in the garage would attract too much attention, so she would need a different vehicle, but first she had to figure out where she was going. Other than breaking out and regaining her freedom, what were her long-time goals? Where would Rand be? Was it safe to try to contact him? She knew what his mission was, and she knew where the mines were, as she had found a road map in the garage.

She could plot a route, but where would she get fuel? She was over a thousand miles away from Kansas City. Before the war it would have been a painless but boring eighteen-hour trip. Now, it could take forever. Any road that went through a city would be destroyed, and she wondered if the cities themselves were a dead zone or if it was safe to travel through the various ground-zero sites.

She decided to explore the subdivision starting at 0230 and return to her safe house at 0430. She wondered if the other houses also had full pantries, and she prayed that at least one house had a usable car and weapons. This was Arizona, surely a few of these homes had weapons.

The odor in the first house she'd broken into stopped her at the door. It was the smell of rot and death. She wrapped her face with a towel she found next to the sink, and when she entered the master bedroom, the cause of the smell was obvious. On the nightstands were lines of empty pill bottles, and on the bed were the decomposing bodies of a man and a woman. Gold assumed they were man and wife, lovers to the end, she thought. They had been holding hands when they slipped away. She thought they must have had nowhere to go, so they decided they'd go across the rainbow bridge together. Gold wondered if she'd find the same situation in the rows of other houses. She prayed she didn't find the bodies of children.

Her prayers weren't answered, because the next house had the bodies of three children and their parents. She couldn't even begin to guess the names of the dead children. She didn't have the time to bury them, so she promised herself she would torch the house when she left to find Rand. She knew Rand could make everything better for her; she didn't understand why, but she felt he could help her. She checked the garage and laughed when she saw two new Teslas sitting there, still connected to their chargers. She knew they were useless, because the national charging network would never be finished now; you could say that the debate between EV and ICE vehicles was settled. ICE won because EVs needed the grid which was a mess with only a small percent of it still functioning.

The third house she tried had a locked door; clearly whoever had lived in it had locked the door before they left. She broke the window next to the back door, reached in, and unlocked the door by turning the lock lever. She looked around and smiled. This house won the jackpot: a weapons' safe and a mid-80s Pontiac Grand Prix. The Pontiac started up after three attempts. She decided to leave the car where it was while she siphoned gas from other cars in the subdivision. She filled every gas can she found. The weapons' safe was going to be a harder nut to crack, but then she remembered what her dad had told her: "People worry they'll forget the combination to their safes, so they usually always write them in a place only they would know.

Gold stood in the middle of the family room where the safe was located, *if I lived here, where would I hide the safe's combination?* After searching four rooms, she discovered it was written on the back of the dry bar in the family room. The numbers had been written on the bottom of the shelf that held a dozen glasses. She memorized the numbers and direction of the turn of the large lock knob. She was rewarded with an unlocking on her first try. She pulled open the door. *I hit the jackpot: two ARs, two pump shotguns, and two Glock 19 9 mm pistoles.* There were also metal boxes full of ammo. As she pulled out the ARs, she noticed two Kbar knives and a small personal first aid kit. She reached up to the shelf above the rifles. *I have my choice of a red dot or a LPVO. I think I'll take the LPVO, and I'll take all of the guns. As I was always taught, one equals none, and two equals one. When you need one the most, it will jam or break. I'm now ready to bring the fight to the enemy. The only thing I need to know is who is my enemy? Who screwed with me? I know Rand will know, but I don't know how to contact him.*

Gold froze when she heard a car slowly driving along the subdivision's streets. *Who are they? Are they looking for me? If they get out of their car, I'll kill them and steal it. It will most likely have a working radio in it.* Gold watched the police car creep past the house she was hiding in. *Ha, they're just doing a drive-by. I guess good help is hard to get. They won't see anything driving along the street. Do they think I'm a raw recruit?*

Gold waited two hours without seeing the police car return before she checked the fourth house. *The stink of death is higher in this house. I'll check the garage and then be gone. Holy shit! One of them was a sheriff. They took their car home at night.* Gold opened the driver's door. *Light still comes on, and the shotgun is in its mount. Radio lit up. I better turn it off.* In the trunk she discovered cop body armor, an M4, and a can filled with loaded magazines. *There's also a large first aid kit and spike strips. The stench of death has most likely gotten into the cotton of the uniform. Maybe I can air the uniform out; that's assuming it fits.*

She found a man and a woman who'd been shot to death. The officer shot her husband and then herself. *I found the uniforms; all I need is the blouse and I'll take her badge and gun. God is smiling on me, there are two uniform blouses in sealed plastic bags. I think I'm going to be a sheriff. I always liked to play dress up.*

The moon was covered by dense clouds as she packed everything she could into the sheriff's trunk and took off toward Kansas City in search of Rand.

*****

Rand sat in the web seat in the almost silent helicopter wondering where Gold had gone. *They're counting on me to know or at least have a good idea where she went. We'd never discussed where one or the other would run to if we had to hide from the powers that be. Where would she have gone? How can I tell them something I don't have any knowledge of? The Secretary is counting on me, and I'm about to let him and her down. I know she needs me, but where is she? A better question is, where would I go if I were in her shoes? I'd hide in plain sight. Where is a good hiding place in plain sight?*

*****

General Thomas Jefferson (he claimed to be related to the famous Confederate general, but there was no proof and some thought he had taken the name because he idolized the Civil War general who'd led the South against the North), assembled his troops and gave them the order to set up an ambush at a blind curve fifteen miles before the entrance to the mines. Of course, Jefferson didn't know he'd picked the same ambush location as another Warlord and the Texas

Rangers. Jefferson's troops were made up of a strange mix of former members of the Kansas and Oklahoma National Guard, armed citizens who recognized Jefferson's authority, and bikers and associated gang members. Jefferson led his troops to the ambush site.

Being the first to arrive, he had his choice of the best ambush sites. He ordered his men and women to dig fox holes, and he had a small team in Jeeps drag trees and large rocks to place in front of the fighting holes to provide some cover. A third of the fox holes had tree logs laid over the top, protecting the soldiers from shrapnel and falling mortar rounds that would explode on the thick coverings.

Jefferson arranged for his field kitchen to prepare a hot meal for his people. He knew that in some cases it would be their last one, and he didn't want it to be MREs. Unfortunately, what Jefferson didn't realize was that the wind carried the scent of the roasting beef after he'd shot a cow that his mess staff had skinned and turned into monster steaks.

The Letts smelled the sweet scent of the roasting beef as did the Texas Rangers who were half a mile behind Letts. The smell made their mouths water, they remembered past steaks they'd eaten in expensive steak houses that no longer existed. Letts' scouts checked the roads leading up to the blind curve. Letts ordered her scouts to slow down and be as quiet as possible, as she knew there was another group there. She wanted her scouts to figure out who they were and to size up their strength. She didn't want to go to war with a potential ally.

Three hours later, the LT in command of the scouts reported, "Ma'am, there is another Warlord here. They've even set up a field kitchen, and half a mile behind their foxholes is a MASH unit."

"Have you been able to ID them or their commander?" Letts kicked the dirt in frustration while looking at her mortar commander. "I guess it's time for me to go meet the competition. Keep your tubes ready. I'm going to keep my radio live; if you hear me say the word, red, I repeat red, then drop HP and WP on them."

Letts got into her up-armored HUMVEE and slowly drove to meet her competition. She wondered who it was. While Letts was thinking of what she wanted to say to the other Warlord, she received a message telling her the Texas Rangers were parking and their commander was walking toward the Warlord who'd already set up his troops at the ambush site. Letts wondered how the Rangers had beaten her here. Letts watched the two men chat. She told her driver to speed up and get her to the meeting before the other two could divide up the best spots and the subsequent spoils. She decided she might have to kill both of them if they didn't agree to cut her in. She very much wanted the President taken alive, and she didn't plan on sharing him with anyone. If that meant she had to kill the other two, then so be it. Letts connected to her snipers. "When I say the word blue, I want you to drop the two standing to your two o'clock. Can you see them? Can you make the shot?"

The snipers radioed back, "Yes, ma'am, we see them, and it will be an easy shot."

"When I say blue, drop them and anyone who jumps up to help them."

"Will do. When you say blue, we'll drop them."

Letts walked toward the other two commanders. "Looks like a party. Didn't you know I'd show up? I've already claimed this spot of land."

Jefferson smiled at Letts. "Look who decided to join us, if it isn't the Warlord of the swamps."

Letts smiled and held out her right hand to shake hands with Jefferson and the Texan Ranger who hadn't introduced himself. He was a mystery, and she didn't like mysteries. I would have been very BLUE if I wasn't invited to the party."

Jefferson figured the word blue was code, and he fell to the ground as the sniper's point 336 round struck his new friend in his head and it blew apart like a watermelon. Jefferson's quick move saved him, as the bullet that had his name on it hit one of his LTs. He looked at Letts. "Neat trick if you can pull it off."

Letts smiled and laughed. "I would have taken both of you out had you not fallen flat on your face like the snake that you are. If you surrender to me, I'll let you live." A moment later a point 308 round struck the tree Letts was standing next to. "Your sniper needs practice. Want to see how a real sniper doesn't miss?"

"No, I have a better idea. Why don't we work together?"

"That's something I'll give some thought to. Who would be the overall commander?"

"One of us is laying in the dirt and the other is standing above, so who do you think earns the position of commander?"

Chapter 19

The co-pilot of the helicopter told Rand to pick up the handset and press line number one because someone wanted to speak with him. Rand said, "Hello, this is Major Rand."

"Major, this is the Secretary of Defense traveling with the President. Do you understand why you were pulled from your company and sent to the base?"

"Sir, I understood you want me to help locate Captain Gold. But sir, I have no idea where she would go."

"Major, I know the two of you have been sharing your sleeping bag, I didn't object as she wasn't a direct report and when she was transferred to your command you've played it by the book. You know her better than anyone else. She has no surviving family. She was making an excellent recovery, and we had hoped she could help us locate Letts' base."

"Sir, she and I do have a relationship, however, we never discussed where one of us would go if we had to escape from a Warlord."

"Son, you know her better than anyone, if you were in her shoes, where would you go?"

"Sir, I've been racking my brain since I received your order to return and assist in locating her. The only thing that comes to mind is that she would try to reach me."

"We've considered that, so we sent drones up to search the potential routes, and we came up empty."

"Sir, which routes did you check?"

"The route you used..."

"Sir, she wouldn't use that route, as she would have had to pass through the Native American border station. If she broke out of the hospital, she clearly doesn't want to be caught and sent back to the same place, so she will use a route that takes her around their territory."

"Major, that's exactly why I ordered you to assume command of the search. You just proved that you do know her better than anyone at the hospital, and that includes her doctors. I've just issued orders that you have the authority to act in my name to use any assets we have to locate her."

"Sir, do you really believe she knows where Letts' HQ is?"

"We do. Her doctors believe it is locked in her mind. Her fog was lifting, and she was remembering things. An example of that is when she remembered her relationship with you. I agree with you that she is most likely trying to reach you."

"Sir, she'll change cars."

"I know. I took the same course as the two of you. I know she'll change cars, but where would she find one? There aren't that many working cars around since the war."

"Sir, she would look for an abandoned subdivision. She would be looking for food, water, first aid materials, a weapon, and of course a working vehicle. Her odds of finding those items increase with the number of empty houses in the subdivision. She'd look for a subdivision that was in the path of the fallout."

"Major, that's what I'm talking about. Find that subdivision and bring our captain back to the hospital so we can get the location of Letts' HQ."

"Sir, I of all people who've lost people to Letts understand how important it is to locate her HQ, but if the doctors use drugs, she may close up and associate the doctors with what Letts did to her."

"Another smart catch. Major, find her, protect her, and get her to tell you where that bitch's HQ is."

"Sir, I'll try."

"I don't want to hear try – just get it done."

The connection was broken before Rand could respond. He made a list of the things he'd want, the first being a map of the fallout clouds and the housing subdivisions that were under the cloud."

Two captains stood at attention when Rand climbed out of the helicopter. He told the pilot to hang around because he might need a ride. When the pilot began to protest, Rand reminded him that he would have the Secretary issue the same order and that it would end up in his 201 file, because they refused an order from a major acting on the direct order from the Secretary. The pilot cut the engine and told one of the ground crew to get his bird refueled and armed with two Hellfire missiles.

A little while later, Rand ran back to the helicopter. "Here are three subdivisions. I need to check each one out. Let's take them in reverse order. We'll start with the one the furthest and work our way back here."

Rand climbed into the bird, and it was airborne before he'd buckled himself in. "When we arrive at the first subdivision fly slowly around it. I'm looking for any signs of someone being there."

"Yes, sir. Sir, you know that the Master Sergeant is going to be really pissed you kept his bird."

Rand smiled. "Tell him to take it up with the Secretary.

Gold left the sixth house she broke into in the gold prize, a diesel-powered pickup. She figured it would be easier to locate diesel than gasoline. She took six of the five-gallon containers of gasoline in case she had to block her path. Five gallons of gas combined with a few of the other chemicals she took with her would be a potent combination. In addition to the jars of chemicals, she took six, ten-pound propane tanks. She also took one of the shotguns, two of the ARs, and two pistols, as well as all of the ammo she could jam into the passenger footwell. She propped an AR on the passenger seat and one of the sidearms on her lap. She had discovered over one hundred silver dollars and twenty gold five-dollar coins in the gun safe. She took them thinking they could be used to barter for fuel.

*****

Rand looked at a tablet the co-pilot had given him, and it showed the images from the cameras under the bird. They flew as slowly as the helicopter could fly, so Rand could look at the doors and windows of every house. After three trips around the subdivision, he told the pilot to take him to the next one.

Rand noticed a broken window by a back door in a house midway around the subdivision. "Land in front of that house," he said, then slowly walked to the rear of the house. He noticed boot prints in dried mud by the back door, and he found the rear door unlocked. He discovered the empty gun safe, and empty cans of chicken breast on the counter. He smiled, *she was here. She loves chicken breasts cut up and mixed with 'Miracle Whip.' She had three cans and some Special K cereal. I bet she didn't sleep here, as there's no indication of her sleeping on the couch, and the beds have the bodies of the dead family in them.*

Rand checked the other nearby houses, and then he called the pilot. "I'm on my way back. We're looking for a white Ford F-150; a work truck powered by a diesel."

Rand called the base drone office. "I want a few drones looking for a white F-150. Check the roads I've marked on the map I just sent you."

"Major, you lack the authority to order me to launch a handful of irreplaceable drones."

"Do I? Well, why don't you take a look at the copy of the form I left with you? I have the Secretary's power to use any assets at our disposal."

"Major, I'm very sorry, but the answer is still no."

Rand placed another call. "Mr. Secretary, I'm sorry to bother you but the drone office refuses to release some of the drones to me. I know what she's driving and where..."

Rand heard what he thought was gunfire.

"Mr. Secretary, are you okay?"

"Major, we're under fir—"

Rand tapped the pilot. "Take us to this position, the president's convoy is taking fire!"

"Yes, sir. You better hold on tight; this baby can really move."

"Then kick her in the ass, time isn't on side. I hope you loaded ammo for the guns, we're going to need them to save the President."

*****

Letts had killed the Rangers' commander; she told the Rangers they could either join her or she would give them five minutes to clear of the area before she ordered them shot by her snipers. They decided to stay with her and accept her as their new commander.

Letts' scouts reported that the President's convoy was approaching their position. "They don't have any armor with them. All we see are technicals and black SUVs. We are guessing the SUVs are armored against rifle fire."

"Letts smiled. "Use your RPGs to knock out the first and last two so they can't move forward, or backup then rack the convoy with your rifles. Your M16s most likely won't penetrate their armor, but you will keep everyone inside their vehicles. Don't let them escape, I'm bringing the majority of our people to your position."

"Yes, ma'am. We'll lock them down."

"Don't forget, I need the president alive. ALIVE! Do you understand me? ALIVE!"

"Ma'am, but if he attempts to escape?"

"Shoot him in his lower legs, but whatever you do, do not kill him."

Jefferson nodded his head. "Excellent orders: simple, clear; something anyone could understand. Will they follow your orders to the letter?"

Letts smiled and nodded her head. "They will, because they can either be rewarded, or tortured to death. I believe they'll choose to be rewarded."

Jefferson nodded. "Good choices."

Letts thanked Jefferson. "How do you motivate your people?"

"I have their families and they know I'll do some really sick stuff to them if they don't follow my orders to the letter. I'd rather they fear me. If they respect me, all the better, but I only really care that my orders are followed."

The President and I were studying the map on my tablet when we saw a flash and felt the ground shake when the lead SUV blew into a large fireball. Before I could say the word 'AMBUSH,' the last vehicle in our convoy joined the lead one in burning down to its frame. Both had been hit by shoulder-fired anti-tank missiles. The missiles had dual warheads: the first was designed to blow up reactive armor, and the second warhead followed directly behind and exploded against the tank's main armor. Their warheads were designed to create a stream of melted copper that burned through the armor and destroyed everything in the tank. Only this time they weren't being used on tanks, they were used against lightly armored trucks and SUVs that didn't have reaction armor. In this case, the dual warheads acted as one large one. And the trucks turned into a giant fireball when their fuel tanks exploded.

I tapped on the bulletproof partition that separated the President and I from the driver and security officer riding shotgun. The security officer lowered the partition so I could speak to them without having to use the wired intercom. "Can we get out of here?"

"We're looking to see if we can use the center island to get away. They hit the first and last vehicle, boxing us in."

"I assume you've called the base and announced burning arrow?"

"Yes, sir. I placed the call as soon as I saw the smoke trail from the first missile. The quick response is on their way."

"Air support?"

"Attack birds are on their way as are the two alert F-16s. They had to rearm because they were armed for air defense."

"How long?"

"Fifteen minutes."

"Order the first one to get here, they can use their guns until the second is rearmed with air to ground missiles and bombs."

The President looked terrified, "It's going to be okay, we have support on the way."

"I hope they get here before these people kill us.

"They don't want to kill you, they want you alive."

"Why? I don't understand."

I glanced at the reports flowing through my tablet, "My gut says we're facing Letts, the warlord who's causing us so many problems. She wants you alive so she can make a deal with you."

I was interrupted by the secret service agent, "Sir, Major Rand is on his way, he stopped to pick up eight members of Delta in their stealth bird. He should be here in 8 minutes."

I smiled. I'd sort of forgotten about Rand. "Contact Rand and tell him to land behind the ambushers to take some pressure off of us."

"Sir, he said the bird is armed with two Hellfires and a thousand 20 mm rounds. He said that he and the Deltas will drop off on the other side of the hill and the stealth bird will hit the attackers head on until they run out of ammo. By that time the attack birds should be here."

The driver said, "Sir, the center island is too narrow for us. The last vehicle is blocking both of the lanes, and its burning rear is hanging over the shoulder in the center island."

"Get up on the island, even if half of the wheels have to be on the freeway and the other half on the grass. This SUV is heavy enough to push that wreck out of our way. Tell the vehicles in front and behind to join us."

I turned to look at the President. "We only have to hold on for a few more minutes."

"Can Rand really do enough to pull the pressure off of us?"

"I have a lot of faith in the major. He knows what needs to be done. He stopped and picked up reinforcements."

"I don't understand how nine people are going to help us."

"Those eight equal twenty normal men. They're experts, and they know exactly what needs to be done. They'll give the ambushers a real kick in the ass."

The President looked worried. "I hope so."

Letts watched the action through her binoculars. "Those three SUVs are trying to escape. The President must be in one of them."

Jefferson shook his head. "If I was in charge of his security, I'd send those three as a lure to get us to go after them while he sits safe in one of the SUVs trying to move. I suggest we hit a couple of the other SUVs."

Letts shook her head. "I'm in charge here and I know he's in one of those three. I've called our scouts back to block their escape. They'll set up a roadblock that they can't get through. We have to hurry this along. I bet reinforcements are on their way."

Jefferson shook his head. "I don't agree, I want to send our people to take the SUVs still in line before they figure a way out of our trap."

Letts smiled at Jefferson before she pulled her sidearm out and shot him in his face. She kicked his dead body when it landed on the ground. "Idiot. I told you I was in charge." She picked up his tablet and sent a message to his people. "I'm sorry to inform you that General Jefferson was struck by a freak shot fired from the SUVs. Prepare to attack them and avenge the murder of the general."

I saw them popping up from their fighting holes, and I knew they were going to rush us. I picked up my tablet and sent a message to each team. "Open the sunroofs and hit them with your 40 mm grenades and full auto. Spray bullets at them."

A moment later, six people stood on their seats and opened fire at the running attackers who were shocked by the counterfire. The grenades came as a rude surprise too. As they were trying to avoid the grenades, they received another surprise: Rand and the eight Delta Operators popped up behind them and opened fire at them. Then a dull gray, almost silent helicopter, unlike something they'd ever seen before, opened fire with its 20 mm cannon.

Letts thought to herself, *I was going to have to kill his followers anyway, so they're doing me a favor. As soon as that bird leaves, I'll send my people to stop the three SUVs after I set off two IEDs that destroy the leading one. I know he's in one of those SUVs, and I'm betting it's the middle one.*

Letts sent a message to her top agents to sneak up to the middle SUV. "Get in there and grab the President. Shoot anyone with him."

Two F-16s suddenly screamed over the battle and dropped their bombs on the now-empty foxholes and the hillside before they went vertical and turned to make another run using their 20 mm cannons. A stinger rose up and struck the wing of one of the F-16s. The pilot managed to eject but was shot as he hung under his parachute. The second F-16 pilot turned and went for cover thinking, *damn, where are the A-10s when we need them?*

Ten people swarmed the President's SUV, putting det cord along the rear doors to blow them off of their hinges so they could grab the President. The SUV shook as the rear doors were blown off of the black bullet-ridden SUV. The security officer had opened his window to return fire, but three 5.56 mm rounds struck him in his face, instantly killing him. Two rounds killed the driver, and I was shot twice as four hands yanked the President out of the SUV.

Letts' people tossed IEDs under the surviving SUVs, so that not even their armor could save them. The explosions tossed the 6,000-pound armored cars into the air, killing everyone in them. The President was blindfolded and dragged to a waiting ambulance, then Letts issued the order to retreat as she climbed into her up armored LAV that had been taken from a National Guard armory.

Chapter 20

Rand led the team of eight Delta Operatives as they shot every wounded terrorist they found. They took two captives for questioning, and the rest were given a free ticket to hell. Rand called for his team to join him at the burning SUVs. One of the Deltas yelled, "I've got a live one! He's been shot and has lost a lot of blood."

Rand called the helicopter. "We have a wounded VIP. I think it may be... oh my God."

"Major, is it the President?"

"No, it's the Secretary of Defense, and without a VP, he's the President, so get down here RIGHT NOW! He needs more care than we can give him."

I opened my eyes and smiled, or better put, I tried to smile at the face hovering over me. "Rand, the President, they took the President."

"I thought so. We'll find him."

"Patch me up and I'll stay and help."

Rand looked at some of my injuries. "Sir, you're going to the MASH unit at the base, and since the President is missing, you're the acting President. I will NOT leave you in a potential war zone while you're bleeding all over everything. From this minute on, you won't be alone."

I couldn't move enough to raise my voice, so I waved Rand to me. "The President?"

"We know Letts has him. There wasn't any blood by the door they blew out to grab him, so I have to assume he's okay. I've ordered Delta Operators to find him and call me with the location. I've also called the team at the tunnel to return and help in the search."

"Rangers?"

"Two companies are on birds flying here. They are due in fifteen. They'll provide some raw firepower for when the Deltas stick their noses too deep in the crap pile."

I nodded, "I see you've learned from Crokett; remember he is one of the best we have. Turn him loose. I'm sure he can find the President."

"Will do. I know he knows his stuff. I know he'll find the President, in the meantime, you have to be the acting President. So, get patched up and get to the command center. I'll keep you informed."

*****

Letts led her convoy in a roundabout route to her headquarters. She thought there might be drones watching her, so she planned to drive around until the typical drones ran out of fuel, but there was one drone still flying circles around Letts' convoy. The Global Hawk flew at 30,000 feet, so it couldn't be seen from the ground. It was sending its data to one of the few remaining satellites that relayed images to the command center located at the base. The information was then relayed to Crockett who followed the convoy from a safe distance so as not to be discovered.

The President sat motionless; it was hard to breathe with the bag over his head. He wanted to save his energy in case an opportunity to escape presented itself. He knew they were driving in circles before they arrived at Letts' headquarters, and he knew there were eyes in the sky watching their route. He also knew that the Delta Operators would turn over every rock to find him. He had seen me get shot, but he knew I wouldn't let him down even if I was wounded. He also knew the Delta Operators were the best special forces in the world. All he had to do was drag out the questioning until his rescuers arrived.

The President heard gunshots, the woods being an almost perfect echo chamber. Every discussion about radiation and the odds of them surviving was recorded so Letts could play it back at her leisure.

Letts ordered a stop to refuel the trucks from the cans they carried with them. She told everyone to walk into the woods to take a leak and be back in five minutes. When everyone was back, she dragged the President out. "If you have to take a leak, or even think about taking one, do it now."

"I can't see."

"I'm sure you can feel for your zipper, and you know what your dick feels like, so just take it out and do it."

The President had a good idea from the sound of Letts' voice that she was to his right side, so he turned to the right and peed on her boots. She screamed and cursed at the President. "I ought to make you lick that up, but you might like it. Now put it away and get back in the truck before I have you beaten to within an inch of your life."

The President got back into the truck knowing he had bought Delta some time for them to catch up. He had heard distant gunfire, and some of them were automatic, but he didn't know if it was his rescuers or if Letts' people were using stolen weapons.

Letts screamed, "Everyone back in the trucks, we have to get out of here before they find us. Attention all drivers, split up per plan L-10."

One of the drivers responded, "To the honor of our ancestors."

The crew responded, "May our actions honor our ancestors."

Letts said to the President, "Get as comfortable as you can, we have a long and winding ride ahead of us. Try to get some sleep, the ride will be less boring that way. I'll wake you at our next stop, which should be in six hours."

"Six hours? Can I ask where we're going?"

"You can ask, but I'm not going to answer. I'm sure you'll recognize it when we arrive. For now, I'm going to remove the bag over your head. There's nothing you can see that will help you escape. You'll know where we're going when we arrive. I believe you'd been there once or twice before the war."

"Do I get a hint?"

"Nope. Even if you guessed the right answer, I won't tell you. I like surprising my guests."

"Now I'm a guest?"

"As long as you behave yourself you are my guest. Do you know why I didn't have you killed?"

"Because you need me as a pawn so you can get the government to agree to split the country. That way, you end up being the queen or emperor, or whatever title you want to call yourself. You tried to use Captain Gold as a go between, but she refused so you induced a stroke. When she was of no further use to you, you dumped her on the side of the freeway and bid her goodbye while you worked your backup plan, which was capturing me."

"Very well done. I'm sure your new accommodations will meet with your approval."

"When will you release me?"

"Shortly, and I do mean shortly, after you sign the agreement of separation and the follow-on treaties of mutual defense and trade between our two countries."

"What makes you think I'd sign such an agreement, or if the people in the land you're claiming will want to be part of your little wet dream?"

"You'll understand much more when we reach our destination."

*****

Master Sergeant Crockett looked at the feeds from the Global Hawk, and then he showed them to his team. "Look at them. It looks like they don't have a care in the world. They're stretching their legs and using the woods along the freeway to answer nature's call. They've also let the President out to stretch and pee. Some of them are milling around and smoking. I don't see a rear guard either. Do any of you see one?"

Crockett handed the tablet around so everyone could see what he was seeing, and they all agreed that they couldn't see a rear guard. Crockett said, "What do they know that we don't?"

No one had any idea why the Warlord's troops looked so happy. Crockett pulled up a road map and said, "Wait a minute, look at the road. I bet they're happy because a couple of them have rigged the hillside to blow, and the debris will block anyone like us from coming up behind them. We need to find a way to pop out in front of them instead of following them. Does anyone have an idea where they are going?"

A corporal asked, "Sergeant, may I see your tablet a moment?"

Crockett handed the table to the young man; he was the second youngest on the team. "Sarge, look at what shows up when I expand the view.

Crockett shook his head. "Shit. I didn't see that coming."

"Has anyone seen that thief of a major who stole our bird?"

The corporal replied, "I saw him when they made a gun run on Letts' position. He motioned to the pilot to RTB."

"I know I shouldn't have loaned my bird to him, but Rand is a nice guy as far as majors go. That being said, stealing our stealth bird is going a little too far. Corp, get on the horn and tell the pilot to get his butt here with a full load of fuel and bullets – lots of bullets."

Rand was dropped off and the bird headed over to Crockett's team as fast as possible.

"Do you believe that's really her HQ?" said Crockett.

"Sir, look at the map. It's the only secure facility in their general direction."

Crockett thought about it for a moment. "You don't believe they're heading to D.C.?"

"No, I don't. There are still too many hot zones in the city, and with most of the bridges down, they wouldn't be able to escape if they saw us coming."

Crockett checked the map for the third time. "You really believe that's where they're taking him?"

"It's secure, and it has everything they need."

Crockett paced around the group; it was his way of thinking. "We have to assume they mined the mountains to block the lanes. Corp, find us a workable route; one they're not using so we control where and when we meet them on the field of battle. Remember our motto." The squad smiled and pumped their right arms. "If you ain't cheating, you ain't winning."

"Corp, how are you doing with the route?"

"Check the map app on your tablet."

"Ah, I like it. Listen up everyone. The Corp is now promoted to Sergeant and is appointed as our official navigator."

One of the staff sergeants asked, "Boss, can you promote him? You're not an officer."

Crockett smiled. "I work for a living. I love everyone, and any I don't, I just..."

The entire squad chimed in, "Kill. You kill anyone you don't like or who pisses you off."

"Let's saddle up. We've got a long and hard journey. If they continue to stop and we don't, we should be able to beat them there."

The squad was on the road within a minute. Crockett told the radio tech to make sure his bird brought them a fuel bladder and lots of ammo and MREs they could give to the locals.

The pilot texted to confirm they were fully loaded, and they were bringing them a hot meal that was being kept warm in insulated cases. The squad was happy at the thought of real food, even though they knew the Master Sergeant wouldn't allow them enough time to enjoy it properly. Crockett kept looking at the map and his watch, then he hit the driver. "Can this thing go any faster?"

"Yes, but we're going to need a second drop of fuel before we reach the exit. I don't want to have to be rationing fuel if we need to hit them and run."

"I'll call for another fuel drop. Haul ass as if you didn't have to worry about fuel. Our first goal is to retrieve the President, and if we have time, I want the Warlord's head on a spike. If she thinks she can kidnap the President out from under my nose, she's got something else coming for her."

Crockett plotted the route and knew it was going to be a real race to see who reached the shelter first. He knew that if Letts beat them to the security all bets would be off the table. He pushed every driver to keep up with his truck, and to stay off of the radio except to report an emergency or an enemy sighting. He thought that Letts might have radio intercept ability. He didn't want her to have access to any information, unless he wanted to give her some fake news.

Chapter 21

Rand ordered the pilot to stop just outside of the MASH unit. He'd radioed ahead to tell them to prepare to receive the Secretary, who was now the acting President. Doctor Hand met the helicopter along with three nurses. He performed an examination of the Secretary, while I had already passed out from the loss of blood and pain. When I opened my eyes, I caught the image of a mask being placed on my face. I couldn't speak or even understand what was happening.

The next time I opened my eyes, I was in a hospital room hooked up to machines that monitored my breathing, my heart, my blood pressure, and my blood oxygen level. I had an IV in each arm. I noticed two armed guards standing in my room and I assumed there were others in the hall.

I needed to know what had happened to the President. I waved one of the guards to me. "Is the President safe?"

"Sir, I don't have any information on the President. My orders are to not allow anyone into your room unless they're on my list."

"Where is Major Rand?"

"I don't know."

"Send someone for him."

"Sir, I wouldn't know where to direct them."

"Get me your commander."

"Yes, sir."

I didn't have any idea how long I waited before a captain entered my room. I knew he wasn't a REMF because he wore a well-worn ABU and not a dress uniform. I checked his name badge. "Captain Golden are you the commander of the guards guarding me?"

"Mr. President, I am. What can I do for you?"

"I'm not the president yet. I have faith that President is still alive."

"Sir, even if he is alive, he isn't here. He isn't in any position to issue orders or run the county. Without a Vice President, or Speaker of the House, or Senate Leader, the position falls to you."

"I don't want it."

"It doesn't matter what you want. If you don't want to be President, then bring the rightful one back."

"Do we know who has him and where he is?"

"Warlord Letts has him, and he hasn't arrived at the location where we assume he'll be held for ransom."

"How do you know he hasn't arrived at his prison yet?"

"Sir, because we haven't heard anything from her yet."

"That's a good reason. Is Major Rand still in camp?"

"Sir, I don't know the Major. Should I send someone to search for him?"

"Please. It's urgent that I speak with him as soon as possible."

"Sir, I'll send some men to search for him."

"Please hurry."

I laid back in the bed and said a silent prayer. *Lord thank you for the third or was this the fourth chance to get it right? I've lost count of how many times you've saved me. I guess you aren't finished with me yet. Lord, please protect the President because that's a job I really don't want. It's one I'm not prepared to carry out. I'm not a politician, I'm a soldier.*

I drifted to sleep when a hand gently touched mine. I opened my eyes. "Rand, good to see you. I need you to do me a favor."

"Sir, anything. It's good to see you recovering."

"I understand I have you to thank for that. The surgeon told me had you not gotten me to the OR when you did, I wouldn't be here, and there would be a fight over who would be President."

"Sir, what can I do for you?"

"Colonel, I want you to find and help rescue the President."

"Colonel?"

"I just promoted you to full colonel. If I got jumped a number of ranks, I could do the same for the person who saved my life and maybe the country. I need you to hook up with Crockett and locate and save the President. While you're doing that, if you also take out or capture Letts, I will give both of you some serious bonus points."

"Sir, how about you agree not to give us any bonus points? I'm not interested in being a general and I know for a fact that the Master Sergeant would resign rather than be promoted to an officer rank."

"Just save him, or I'll make your nightmare come true and promote you to flag rank. Then I'll make you my aide. The last time I tried to promote you to that position, you weaseled out. Something about saving Captain Gold, who I note is still missing."

"Sir, I believe she's looking for me."

"Excellent, I may be able to kill two birds with one shot. You can remind Crockett that if the two of you fail in this mission and I have to sit behind that desk, I'll promote Crocket to a butter bar and won't accept his or your resignation. There's still a war on, so neither of you can resign without my permission."

"Yes, sir. I better be on my way."

One of the guards ripped the oak leaf off of Rand's blouse and pushed on the patch of a full colonel. "Sir, congratulations."

"I thought he hadn't told anyone. I thought I could escape it but he told you to dig me up the rank patch, didn't he?"

"Yes, sir. You're going to see a lot of me. I've been assigned as the commander of your protection detail."

"LT, good for you. I hope you know what you signed up for."

"I did, and I also alerted the pilot to return the bird, fuel it up, and arm it. He's down and will be ready to go by the time we reach the flight line."

The pilot looked pissed that he'd been called back to the base to pick up a colonel; that was until he saw that the colonel was none other than Rand. "Sir, it looks like congratulations are in order."

"It wasn't my idea. Captain. When will you be ready?"

"As soon as you buckle yourself in, we're off."

"Captain, what's the range of this bird?"

"Colonel, a normal Blackhawk has a range of 362 miles, but we carry more gas in the two additional tanks, so we can make it to an even 500 miles."

"Then I hope we have a refueling site up and running. We need to pick up the Master Sergeant and his team."

"Sir, we can't fit all of them in this bird, so I ordered two additional birds to follow us."

"Are they like this one?"

"One is, and the other is a regular bird. There were only a handful of these made, I think there were four and here are two of them. I think one was destroyed when the Mountain was nuked."

"I assume you've arranged fuel for us."

The pilot smiled. "Yes, sir. I used your rank to get the refueling sites up and waiting for us. I planned three stops and then another just before we reached the target. That will give us enough fuel in case we have to go into attack mode or dodge MANPADs."

Rand asked, "Wait one minute, where did a Warlord get their hands on MANPADs?"

"Same place they got all of their other weapons and gear: they went shopping at every Guard armory in their area. They either found the person who had the key to the armory, or they used torches to cut their way in."

Rand slowly nodded. "That means they most likely have mortars too."

The pilot nodded. "Assume they have everything they could carry or load onto trucks from the armories. MREs, weapons, trucks, construction equipment and of course, anti-tank and anti-air missiles. I bet at least a couple of the armories were loaded to the gills because they were tasked with going to the Sand Box before we left all those niffy toys behind."

"Did any WMD end up here?"

"No idea, but anything is possible. We've had years of an open border where a nuke could have been carried across the river and blown one of our cities off the map; that's before the Russians did them a favor and did it before the terrorists could have acted."

"You're saying there are loose nukes here?"

"I really don't know. I do know that there are hundreds of weapons bunkers that could be opened with the right tools. Think about all of the crap stored in those bunkers. There are hundreds just waiting for someone to open them. Granted, many are Air Force bombs, but as we learned in the War on Terror, they make perfect IEDs."

Rand nodded his understanding. "Then we better stop Letts before she learns of them and uses them against us. I'm ready when you are."

The three helicopters leaped into the air and flew east in a "V" formation, the regular Blackhawk at the point and the two stealth birds making up the arms of the "V."

*****

Captain Gold stopped at every truck stop to take fuel cans that she siphoned diesel into. She loaded the pickup with a total of one hundred gallons of diesel. Combined with the truck's full tanks, she figured she could find Rand. She knew where he was going to the mines under Kansas City. She had taken a road map from the truck stop so she would know not only the most direct route, but also the surface roads in case the freeways were blocked.

She had taken a few 'walkie-talkies' from a sporting goods store that had managed to avoid getting lotted. She also took a box of batteries from the truck stop. She didn't know what frequency, or the range of the small radios used, but she hoped that at least one would be the same as used by the army and that it had the range to reach her major. She placed the radios on the passenger seat and on the back seat, hoping at least one of them would speak to her.

She hadn't seen another soul in two hundred miles. She knew she had driven through the dead zones. In vast areas, the fallout had killed every living being. She was tired after having driven for eleven hours. She decided to find an abandoned house to take a nap in. Luck smiled on her because she saw a farmhouse with a large barn on the side of the freeway. The fields were littered with carcasses of dead cows, pigs, and horses. She pulled into the gravel driveway, and she opened the barn door and parked the truck inside so no one could see it. She attached an ankle holster with a small Ruger LCP Max pistol on her right ankle and covered it with her uniform pants. Then she checked the chamber of one of the AR pistols. She had assumed the owner hid it in her safe, thinking the ATF would never go house to house looking for whoever had stashed away the once-outlawed weapons. She wondered if the owner knew the Federal Courts had overruled the ATF. It didn't matter anymore because the ATF no longer existed.

This one had a 7.5" barrel and was loaded with subsonic 300 Blackout rounds. The heavy 220 gr bullets were deadly at ranges inside of 100 yards. She knew that if she had to use it, it would most likely be within 50 yards, so the large bullets were perfect for defending herself. She wished she had a suppressor that would have made the firing almost silent. The sight was a small red dot that made targeting a simple task.

She knocked on the back door, and she wasn't surprised that no one answered, she hadn't expected them to. She pushed the door open and was again hit with the smell of death. Two seniors had been holding hands until they passed away.

She grabbed some blankets, a pillow, and three bottles of water; she had decided she would sleep in the barn. She didn't expect anyone would be poking around because most people were still afraid of the fallout. So, they either left for safer areas or they arranged to take their own lives rather than suffer the pain of radiation poisoning.

She opened her eyes and was surprised to see she'd slept for eleven hours. She used the well to wash up, and loaded as much canned food as she could fit into the pickup with the fuel. She'd discovered the rows of canned food on shelves in the barn, and two cases of bottled water were piled under the shelves. She filled most of her five-gallon fuel containers from the farmer's supply he had used to fuel his tractor. She made sure no one was watching as she pulled the pickup out of the barn. Within three minutes, she was back on the freeway. The going was slow due to the thousands of abandoned vehicles everywhere. She said to herself, *too slow, too many abandoned vehicles. People either died in them or they just left them and sought a safe location.*

*****

Crockett asked his staff, "Where is our bird? We need it to cut off Letts."

His Sergeant replied, "Colonel Rand has taken it over in addition to her sister and another Blackhawk. He's also bringing us the rest of our team and some Rangers."

"Colonel? I wonder whose ass he kissed. He was a captain a month ago, and now he's a damn LT Colonel?"

"No. He's a full bird colonel."

"WTF? What am I doing wrong?"

His best friend smiled. "I heard you were offered a promotion and turned it down."

"I work for a living. Do I look like or act like a damn officer? Where is the good colonel taking my bird?"

"Sarge, he's on his way here."

"With all three birds?"

"Yes."

"Remind me not to bad mouth the Colonel again, or at least not in front of him. Make sure one of you reminds me to watch my mouth. I can't believe he's on the short path to flag rank. Oh well, it shows you all that any of you could become an officer, but do any of you actually want to be an officer? Let me know and I'll put the papers in. Then I'll salute you and joke about you behind your back. I'll be able to say I knew the SOB way back when." The operatives laughed. None of them cared much for becoming an officer.

"Let's make sure we have a nice marked landing place for the Colonel; we wouldn't want to be chewed out for not being prepared for his arrival. As soon as he lands, Team A is going to board the three birds while Teams B and C will take the vehicles and race across the mountains. I want to be very clear: stop for no one. Each truck has three people so you can rotate drivers. You must keep to the schedule. If you come to a roadblock, blast your way through it. All that matters is that we meet at the target together so we can strike it from the front entrance and the hidden one I've marked on the map. Does anyone have any questions?"

A corporal asked, "What happens if we get there and Letts and the President aren't there?"

Crockett nodded. "An excellent question, but take my word for it, they will be there. It's the safest and most secure place they can go. They need a place where they can communicate to give us their terms. It's the only place within hundreds of miles that is both secure and has the equipment to communicate with us."

*****

Captain Gold drove during the day and slept at night. She was afraid her headlights would draw too much attention to her because they could be seen for miles. She also didn't want to risk hitting a wild animal that may damage the radiator or the engine. She didn't know if her luck would hold out and she'd be able to locate another usable truck.

She saw the burned and broken sign announcing she had entered Oklahoma hours ago when one of the radios on the passenger seat buzzed. Static filled the interior of the truck when she heard a voice... a voice she thought she'd never hear again. "Sitrep for Able Six Actual."

Rand said, "This is Able Six Actual, send it."

"Landing spot per red smoke, confirm birds."

"We see red smoke, three birds, two S type and one Blackhawk."

The next sentences were unintelligible from the static. Gold said to herself out loud, "At least I know he's alive and in command, but I don't know where they are. I don't see any smoke yet. I don't think the President would change his orders though, so I guess they're still on their way to the mines. All I have to do is follow the route we would have used before and I'm sure I'll run into them."

Gold rolled her window down and leaned her head out. "I thought I heard a Blackhawk." She stopped and got out so she could focus on the sound she thought she'd heard. She looked up and saw a Blackhawk leading two very strange looking helicopters. They were almost silent. "What in the world are they? Are they Russian or Chinese? I didn't see any country markings on them. Damn the radio. This close he's got to hear me."

She rushed back to the truck and grabbed the radio that had picked up the previous conversation. "Captain Gold for Major Rand, repeat, Captain Gold for Major Rand."

The co-pilot said to Rand, "Someone is using our network to ask for you as Major Rand."

"Have you asked for the daily code?"

"Yes, sir. They said they had been away from the base for a while and didn't know the daily code."   Rand asked, "Man or woman on the radio?"

"Sounded like a woman. They said they were Captain Gold."

"Ah, I bet that was our favorite Warlord, Sharon Letts. She must be trying to figure out where we're going. Don't respond to her again and send a message to

Crockett to change frequencies to the backup. Let's hope she doesn't know our backup frequency."

All of a sudden, all Gold could hear was static. "Shit, they don't believe me. They most likely thought I was Letts. Damn it, they won't talk to me without the daily code, and I have no way to know the code. I will have to chase them down so I can speak with them face-to-face. Once they see me, they'll know I'm not the Warlord. Maybe I can reach them before they take off, then I'll see Rand and he'll recognize me. Everything will be like it used to be. I have to hurry. Those birds can fly in a straight line."

*****

Crocket snapped to attention when Rand jumped out of the helicopter. The Delta Operators all followed his lead and saluted the colonel. "Master Sergeant, don't give me that BS."

"Colonel, I am showing your shiny new Eagles the respect they deserve."

Rand returned the salute. "Okay, now that we've gotten that over with, I thought you'd be pleased I didn't destroy your bird, and I even brought you its twin and a Blackhawk for transport. I couldn't get hold of any more though. Even a shiny new Colonel can't easily steal a half dozen helicopters. I did make sure these are armed and loaded with ammo."

"Colonel, I do thank you for returning my bird fully armed. What are we going to do about fuel? We've got a long way to go."

"Fuel bladders have been placed at these positions. Each is guarded by two squads."

Crockett smiled, "Those eagles really have some pull. I'm very impressed."

Rand smiled. "One question: do you know where we're going? Where are they taking the President?"

"To the one place that's going to be a real pain to break into; the one place designed to keep people like us out."

"I'll bite because I don't have any idea where such a place is after the war."

"Colonel, let me show you on the map where we're going."

"Crockett you've got to be shitting me. There's not a snowball's chance in Hell that that facility still exists. Surely the Russians targeted it. It's most likely a hole in the ground. Camp David and Site R were destroyed. Why would they have spared this one?"

Crockett smiled. "Colonel, they didn't spare it. Their missile missed."

"Missed a target that large? Where did it land?"

"In the ocean. I understand it created a huge tsunami that washed radioactive water for miles inland. Towns that were spared from the nukes died under the dirty water. The wind picked up the water vapor and carried it for hundreds of miles."

Rand thought for a minute. "The Russians once had monster-sized nukes they planned on exploding along our coasts. They knew the tsunamis would kill millions and the winds would carry the radiation across the country. It's a good thing for us that the ones that exploded along the West Coast weren't the monster ones we were led to believe they had, and the ones along the East Coast never exploded because the sub that was supposed to trigger them had been sunk by one of our attack boats."

Crockett asked, "Why didn't they use them?"

"Their attack plan didn't give them time to deploy them. They were afraid we'd get wind of them, and we'd hit them first, so they counted on a decapitating strike to buy them the element of surprise. They figured our slow response time would be enough for their full attack to take out our birds sitting in their silos. They might have succeeded had a General in the Pentagon not given the order for us to launch."

Crockett thought it over for a while, then nodded.

Rand said, "Okay, I'll accept that the Russians missed. Their accuracy was always for shit anyway. It was why they built larger warheads than us. Anyway, so assuming the damn place survived, how would Letts know that?"

Crockett handed a tablet to Rand who skimmed the lines of information. "We ran across her old HQ and discovered some of her files. She had followers in ten states. Some were in the Guard, and some were in the Army. I bet thousands of survivors were also attracted to her message and the offer of food and clean water convinced them to change sides. Some were most likely on the staff of the Guard and maybe even the Army. She most likely has tapped some of our lines. It's the only thing that makes any sense."

Rand asked for a couple of minutes so he could check if any of the known staff had been reporting to the Secretary. "Well, well, it appears we have an informer in the facility. "Letts' convoy hasn't arrived yet. According to our source, she was stuck in the mountains fighting people loyal to the US. Many of them are hunters. They took Letts by surprise. Some of those shooters took them under fire at a distance of a mile."

Crockett looked surprised. "A mile?"

"Yup. And they didn't just hit the vehicles; they took out the people standing at the guns in the pickup beds and anyone standing up exposed. They said that if we're coming, we should let them know and make sure we use the southbound lanes. We should stay out of the northbound because they have them mined with IEDs. According to the source, Letts should enter the mined zone any minute. I sent the source a warning that Letts has the President. We can't afford to lose him."

Crockett was about to speak when Rand held his hand up to silence him. "The source is asking if we know which vehicle the President is in."

"I'm going to tell them that he is most likely in the same vehicle as Letts."

Crockett asked, "Are you sure? Because if you're not, it could cost him his life. You're playing with fire. The Captain I once knew, knew better than to play with fire. The Major I knew would weigh the odds before jumping in. Now the Colonel who is standing in front of me could be playing with real fire. Fire way over his pay grade."

Rand smiled. "You mean I'm getting paid for this? I hope they pay in precious metal coins. If they made a direct deposit, I'm screwed; my bank and their data center were atomized in the war."

Crockett laughed. "Yeah, I haven't seen a paycheck since the war too. I guess we've got to save the President so he can authorize our pay."

"Yup, I guess we better get going. Any idea how long Letts is going to be held up?"

Rand replied, "No idea. I knew we were going to have to make a fuel stop and it takes time to fuel these beasts. We are going to need Letts slowed down so we can intercept her before she reaches the facility, because if she gets there before us, I'm not sure we can break ourselves in."

Crockett picked up the radio. "Listen up my wayward children, we're going to go save the President so we can get paid."

The corporal smiled. "You mean we're really to get paid? What the hell is left to spend it on anyway?"

Crockett laughed. "Booze and broads."

The corporal joined him. "Count me in."

The three birds were loaded with every operator they could jam into the interior. Rand sat in the co-pilot's seat, while the co-pilot took the trucks. He said he was going to meet them in Virginia.

*****

One of the other radios on the passenger seat of Gold's truck happened to be tuned to Rand's new frequency. She could hear them, and she knew she was gaining on the convoy, and that the President was being held by Letts. She listened to their conversation as she stopped to empty her bladder. Then she traced the route in her map book, until she found what she was looking for: a back road that cut through the mountains.

One that, if she was very lucky, would place her at the facility at the same time as Rand. She didn't know the Colonel that the Delta company commander spoke of, and she didn't understand how Delta was organized. They had a Master Sergeant commanding rather than an officer. She figured it was fine because they didn't have many combat officers left; many had been killed in Ukraine when the Russians hit their bases with nukes, and many others were killed when their bases back home were hit too. She figured if a Master Sergeant was their commander, it was for a reason, and she'd respect and learn from him.

She hadn't heard the story of how the facility had survived, and she had been surprised when she'd learned where Letts planned to keep the President. She smiled, and spoke out loud, "I understand why Letts planned on holding the President there. There was only one way in or out. It's one of the most secure places left in the country. Shit, this is really going to be a race against time, and time isn't on my side." She didn't know about the secret exit. "I have fuel in the cans to see me all the way. My only fear is falling asleep behind the wheel. I thank the Good Lord for sharing these cases of Red Bull. I hate the taste, but between the caffeine and the sugar from the candy bars I found, I'll be so wired I might not be able to sleep for a week. At least I know where Rand is going and why. I don't know where or how I'm going to cross the Mississippi.

"Wait, I don't need to know; I only have to know where the Delta Operators plan on crossing. I'm able to pick up some of their conversations, and the last few words I heard were Alton. It seems the townspeople built or rebuilt the bridge across the river. If it's good enough for Delta, it will be good enough for me. I should reach Alton in five hours. Thankfully, there's no police to catch me as I let this diesel feel its oats and fly at 100 mph when the road is clear. If Letts manages to reach the facility before Rand, it will be almost impossible for us to rescue the President."

She checked the map, and she was only an hour at 100 mph from Alton. "I don't want to race down their main street and possibly kill some of their kids, but if I stop being only one person, I can be easily overwhelmed. I can't risk losing my truck and everything in it. But I have to get across the river and find Rand. He's the only one who can help me. He's the only one I can count on.

I can't believe Mount Weather survived, and Letts has control of it.

*****

Rand sat on the co-pilot's seat, and he closed his eyes and let his mind drift. *Damn Letts and the other Warlords. We can't afford a civil war. We'll need decades, maybe generations, to rebuild. A civil war will throw us into a chaos that we might never recover from. The American dream could die. The Chinese might recover and attack us. Europe is already rebuilding along the lines of their history: feudal kingdoms fueled by self-appointed kings and princes. I don't want that to be our future, but the only way I can see to reverse the tide of history is to recover our President and kill Letts and every other Warlord.*

"Colonel, sorry to interrupt you."

Rand shook himself to full consciousness. "Pilot, what's up?"

"Sir, the Blackhawk is experiencing an overtempt warning on its second engine. We have to put down so the techs can check it."

"How far away is our refueling point?"

"That's where we're trying to reach. We've reduced our speed so the injured Blackhawk keeps up without doing more damage to the engines."

"I'd ask how long the delay will be, but I know you won't know anything until the techs check it out."

"Yes, sir. We're twenty minutes out from our first refueling location. There are troops and techs waiting for us."

"Okay, please keep me informed. I don't need to tell you time isn't our friend. If the Blackhawk can't keep up, we'll have to do the impossible."

Crockett looked at the back of Rand's helmet. "Colonel, do you realize we don't have enough people to take the shelter as it is."

"Master Sergeant, we're called to do the improbable every day. Today we've been called on to do the impossible. I had a chance to read your file; your complete file, and I know you've pulled off similar missions with less people. If I had to walk through Hell to accomplish a mission, I'd want you on my team. I have faith in you and your people."

"Colonel, I wish I had the same confidence as you have in my team."

They were interrupted by the pilot. "Sir, someone is on the horn again asking to speak with you, she claims to be a certain Captain Gold. She doesn't have the daily code word."

"Connect me. I'll get to the bottom of this."

"Captain Gold, this is Colonel Rand, please answer the following questions so I can confirm that you're really Captain Gold. They something that only the two of us would know."

Ten minutes later, Rand shook his head. "It seems impossible, but she is who she claims to be."

Crockett asked, "Are you sure? If it's Letts, we're opening ourselves up to a real problem."

"She knew things that only she and I would know. Even if Letts had managed to break her, she wouldn't have been able to know the answers to my questions. Two were very personal."

"Yes, sir. How far away is she?"

"Too far for her to reach us in time, so while the techs work on the Blackhawk, I want the second stealth bird to pick her up and bring her here."

Crockett exploded, "NO F-CKING WAY! I'm not risking the loss of my second stealth to pick up your girlfriend."

"Crockett, she knows more about Letts than anyone else."

"Damn you, Colonel, if something happens to our stealth bird, you won't have to worry about ever wearing stars."

"Sergeant don't get yourself wound up. The president wants her back, so consider this to be a direct order from the President."

"I consider freeing the president from Letts to be more important. When the Blackhawk is repaired, why not send it? The stealth birds may save our lives."

"I'll agree to that."

Crockett looked surprised, "You mean I won this argument?"

"Yeah, you did. Can you show me your plan to free the President?"

"Yes, we can discuss it on the bird."

"Shit, I know what that means, you're making it as you go." Rand shook his head in disbelief. Crockett just smiled.

End of Book 3

Please follow me on Facebook, my author page is https://www.facebook.com/profile.php?id=100063482926235 to learn up-to-date release dates and other new information about my stories.

Other by the author are available on Amazon:

We're Not Alone. Book 1
We're Not Alone, Book 2 (Coming spring 2024)

NATO's Article 5 Gambit Book 1
NATO's Article 5 Gambit Book 2 The March through Hell
NATO's Article 5 Gambit Book 3 March into Darkness
NATO's Article 5 Gambit Book 4 (Coming early 2024)

Buddy can you spare a few Trillion?

Behind Every Blade of Grass book 1
Behind Every Blade of Grass book 2
Behind Every Blade of Grass book 3
Behind Every Blade of Grass book 4
Behind Every Blade of Grass book 5
Behind Every Blade of Grass book 6
Behind Every Blade of Grass book 7
Behind Every Blade of Grass book 8
Behind Every Blade of Grass book 9
Behind Every Blade of Grass book 10

The Smoky Mountain Militia (A story set in the Behind Every Blade of Grass universe.)
Fighting Behind Enemy Lines. (Coming winter 2024.) (A story set in the Behind Every Blade of Grass universe.)

The Wrath of God, Book 1
The Wrath of God, Book 2
The Wrath of God, Book 3, (coming in 2024)

Red Sunset.
Earthquake

Pestilence
Pax Romana

It's Good to be the King. Book 1
It's Good to be the King, Book 2

The Changelings Book 1
Justin's Journal
Project Xiangqi
Korean Crises

CALEXIT, Book 1, Secession
CALEXIT, Book 2, Politics as Normal.
CALEXIT, book 3, If at First, You Don't Secede

America on Fire

37 Miles (Revised Edition)
37 Miles, Book 2, Patty's Journey

My Story
A History Lesson (Short story)

2015 Second American Civil War, Book 1
2015 Second American Civil War, Book 2
2015 Second American Civil War, Book 3
2015 Second American Civil War, Book 4
2015 Second American Civil War, Book 5

By the Light of the Moon, Book 1
By the Light of the Moon, Book 2
By the Light of the Moon, Book 3
By the Light of the Moon, Book 4

Christmas Eve

The Shelter, Book 1, The Beginning
The Shelter, Book 2, A Long Day's Night
The Shelter, Book 3, The Aftermath
The Shelter, Book 4, The New World.

The Shelter, Book 5, War
The Shelter, Book 6, Revenge
The Shelter, Book 7, Genesis
The Shelter, Chapter 2, a new beginning.

In the Year 2050, America's Religious Civil War
In the Year 2050, Book 2

The Impeachment of President Obama
Silent Death
The Third World War

We Knew They Were Coming, Book 1
We Knew They Were Coming, Book 2
We Knew They Were Coming, Book 3
We Knew They Were Coming, Book 4
We Knew They Were Coming, Book 5
We Knew They Were Coming, Book 6
We Knew They Were Coming, Book 7
We Knew They Were Coming, Book 8
We Knew They Were Coming, Book 9
We Knew They Were Coming, Book 10

Feel free to contact me at itabankin@aol.com with any questions or comments.

Printed in Great Britain
by Amazon

31949429R00076